Time Will Tell

Leah Goldwig

Contents

Prologue

T ime will tell

Don't ever believe a person who says he's perfect. Why? Because nobody is. Everyone makes mistakes, everyone hurts someone whether it be intentionally or unintentionally, everyone lies, everyone has their own demons and everyone has a different life. Some people call others stupid or naive because they love someone who clearly doens't love them back although they have no idea why she loves him or why he loves her. They don't know the reason behind it but they still decide to judge.

Everybody experiences life, love, hurt, pain, happiness and sadness in a different way. While some of us are smarter, more careful, wiser, stronger, less emotional, more experienced, some others simply aren't. Maybe someone has had a rough life and had to deal with a lot of stuff someone else didn't have to. Maybe another one had to carry some heavy weight on his shoulders at a very young age another one didn't have to. How are these people even supposed to understand what someone else went through when they can't identify themselves with their life, their past, their character, their problems?

The only thing I believe everybody has in common is suffering. We all suffer, but in different ways. Some people suffer due to strict diets, some because they may have lost a family member or a loved one due to violence, war or a car accident, some suffer because of heartbreak, others because they think their life is tough and the majority of people suffer from poverty. Every single person on this planet has a reason to suffer — and we do.

As I said, everyone has their own demon. A demon who is constantly by our side just sitting and waiting for the right time to come and get us. He poisons our minds, our brains and our hearts. We change. Maybe we build walls around us to protect us from people, to protect us from getting hurt, to protect us from suffering. But what we don't realize is that the higher we build those walls around us, the harder we fall once the right person walks into our life to tear them down.

I also believe that people have good hearts —some at least. I think that those evil people are the reason as to why good people turn cold, emotionless, reckless, numb. They are the demons no one warned us about. They are the ones who poison us, who change us, who make us suffer, who hurt us.

Sadly, my demon was a girl I deeply loved — but that's exactly how they do it. Love is their greatest and most powerful weapon and they use it against us oh so mercilessly. And unfortunately, she caused me to build walls so high they blinded my clear sight, my clear vision and my clear mind. I build them so high that I was scared to fall again, to trust again, to love again and to be loved again. So high that I didn't even believe that true love and soulmates exsited - until this other girl came along.

...

"You destroyed her," he shouted before he covered his face with both of his hands, while pretending to be outraged.

I nodded slowly as I closed my eyes for a brief moment to collect my thoughts and to stay calm. "That's right. I did. I destroyed her and guess what? That destroyed me even more."

"You broke a perfectly good heart," he stated the obvious again.

"And that broke me completely," I mumbled hoarsely. He was making me angrier each passing second he opened his mouth and I was getting sick by just staring at him and listening to him talk about what Rose and I had although he didn't even have a clue about us.

"Are you serious? No, you can't be. You didn't even love her, let alone care about her a single bit. She suffered so much because of all the things you put her through and—"

"Arg, shut up!" I screamed this time because I couldn't listen to his words any longer. "I know that I put her through hell, I know that I hurt her, I know that I made her feel so much pain. I am aware of that, but don't you dare tell me that I didn't love her! You don't know about us, you don't know anything about—"

"I don't want to! I know everything I need to know about you and that's enough. You are pathetic and I am honestly just disgusted by you." It was his turn to cut me off now and once he finished his sentence, I balled my hands into two fists because my anger was boiling inside of my body. I would feel a lot better if I punshed him and broke his nose or knocked him out while doing so.

I scoffed, rubbing my eyes before I lowered my gaze on him. "Time will tell."

"What do you mean?"

"Time solves most things. Time heals nearly all of our wounds. Time makes us understand what's important in life, it has a beautiful way of showing us what truly matters," I muttered loud enough for him to hear. "Only time will tell."

Chapter 1 - The Party

T ime will tell

flashback

"We don't have to stay until the morning hours, alright?" I assured as I put my hand on top of her own just to give it a tight squeeze. Although Jo didn't want to accompany me at first, I was glad that I managed to convince her successfully.

She looked at me with those beautiful mesmerizing eyes before she pouted. "Can we stay for an hour or two only? I really don't feel good. I'd rather stay home with you, cuddle with you and watch some sappy romance movie with you."

I smiled widely. "Pinky promise we can do all of that and even more tomorrow baby. I didn't feel like coming either, but I had to because of Toby. As I said, we don't have to spend the entire night here. Once we eat our pieces of cake, we leave."

"Okay Miles." She rolled her eyes and kept staring at me before she smiled as well. "You do this for Toby and I do this for you."

"I love you," I whispered loud enough for her to here as I moved closer to place a kiss onto her plump lips.

"I love you, Miles."

Once we walked inside, I realized that the house seemed to be quite empty. I expected a lot more people and a bigger crowd, but as for now it were up to twenty people who were hanging around the house with some red cups in their hands and a few girls by their sides. Jo intertwined her small hand with mine and whispered, "I'll go over to my friends and you can-"

She couldn't finish her sentence because Toby and James came walking towards us and pulled me into a hug which caused me to let go of her hand. "Nice to see you, Miles! Come on over to our table."

I turned my head sideways to look at my gorgeous girl and saw her smiling my way. "Go. I'll be sitting in the living room with some other girls, don't worry."

"We won't stay long," I repeated for the twentieth time.

"It's okay Miles! Just go," she laughed, pushing me forward until James put his arm around my shoulder to guide me into a different direction. Andrew, Mark and Ashton were seated on the table we just reached with some beer, water and coke placed in front of them. We all greeted each other except for Andrew who seemed to be in deep thought but I shrugged it off for now and just squeezed his shoulder.

"Jo is looking like fire tonight," Ashton joked just to upset me although he knew that it didn't bother me anymore. He loved to tease me with Jo only to feel satisfied whenever I threw a tantrum but once I figured out that he said those words to make me angry, I stopped paying attention to them.

"Shut up." I cut him off straight away and he chuckled.

"Girl, girls, girls. Are we going to talk about girls the entire night again? Why do we always talk about girls? Let's talk about football for once, man." Mark puffed with a good amount of annoyance lacing on his deep voice and it was James' turn to be the annoying prick this time.

"Okay, let's talk about something else then," he suggested while staring at Andrew with a malicious gaze. "Andrew, are you still here with us?"

"What's wrong with him?" I asked Toby, keeping my voice low right after James finished his question. If it was a touchy subject, I didn't want them to force Andrew to talk about it.

Toby shrugged nonchalantly. "I honestly don't know. He's been acting this way ever since he arrived."

"Why are you so upset, dude?" James nudged Andrew's sides with his elbow as he brought a glass filled with whiskey to his lips. James was a douche and sometimes I truly hated his guts but he was still a friend of mine nevertheless, so I had to keep up with him and his annoying behavior. "Still no luck in bed with her?"

Andrew swallowed hard as he rolled his eyes before he looked up at James, Toby, Mark, Ashton and I. "None of your business, alright?"

"Wait, what was her name again?" Ravi asked confused once he approached us. Andrew was one of my closest friends because he was the only one I could actually trust out of all of them. He was great at keeping things to himself and listening to all my problems without judging me at all. I mean he knew a lot about Jo and I because I told him about how much my life changed ever since I met her. He was the only decent guy and that's why I liked him.

"It was some flower, I think. Or wait... I don't know," James teased him while covering his mouth with his hand to suppress his stupid laugh. He knew damn well what her name was, she was his number one target at school. He had a crush on her during middle school but she simply never payed any attention to him or to anyone at all. To calm my nerves, I turned my head sideways to look over at Jo and I caught her as she laughed, which caused me to smile to myself like a fool.

With my eyes still set on my girl, I replied, "Her name is Rose." Andrew was way too focused on his drink and avoided to look -let alone talk- to us. I felt bad for him somehow because he has been dating her for a couple of months and sadly didn't have any luck with her. I guess she was an introvert who loved to spend time on her own rather than with her significant other.

I knitted my eyebrows at him as I observed his facial expression. He seemed like he was about to cry and that hurt me too. I have never seen Andrew so vulnerable, so broken and so sad. Then I glanced over at James and asked, "Can you get me another drink?"

"I'm not your bitch, go get yourself another drink," he spat and I had to lick my dry lips wet to stop myself from breaking his nose right here, right now. If it wasn't for Jo, my fist would have already connected with his left cheek, but Jo was not a fan of me getting into fights so I tried to control myself around her a lot more.

"Shut your stupid mouth." I gulped my coke down and averted my gaze towards the ceiling just to avoid looking at his face instead.

"Let's talk about Green Day, maybe Miles stops being a jerk then," he mocked, followed by his obnoxious laugh once again. "Or about how—"

"Enough is enough." I closed my eyes and took a deep breath in before I re-opened them to stare at Andrew again but he couldn't be found on his previous spot and I noticed that he was walking towards the bathroom so I rushed behind.

"Hey," I called after him.

It took him a while but when he turned around to look me in the eyes, I spotted those tears he was trying to hold back. He was obviously hurt, but I had no idea why. "I have to pee, Miles. Please just leave me alone."

"Come on, tell me." I crossed my arms in front of my chest as I leaned my back against the wall behind me. He simply needed someone to talk to and I wanted to be the one to listen to all his problems this time.

"We broke up," he mumbled sadly. "Well, actually I did. I couldn't do it to such a beautiful girl like her.

I pulled my eyebrows together in confusion. "Wait, I thought you loved her?"

He looked to his left and right before he said, "Miles, I already told you that I accidentally cheated. I couldn't look into her eyes or kiss her without constantly thinking about the fact that I cheated!" He raised his voice before he covered his face with both of his shaky hands.

I sighed, rubbing my neck slowly to think about some comforting words to say to him but apparently I wasn't good at this. "You should've told her. If she truly loves you, she will get over it. I mean you were drunk off your ass."

"It was her best friend, do you honestly think she would?" he scoffed. "No, she would't. She never would. I'd rather stay friends with her for now... I mean maybe we could work something out again... in the future."

"Holy shit." I covered my mouth this time as my eyes grew twice their size. "You fucked up big time."

"Yeah, I know. Thank you for reminding me again. I really have to use the bathroom now." And with that he walked away, but I remained at my spot and thought about that girl Rose for a few minutes. Although she was Noel's sister, she was the complete opposite. I never really payed much attention to her, but now I wondered how she managed to turn Andrew's life upside down.

—

The hours were passing by pretty fast and I was sad that I couldn't be around Jo most of the night but we didn't want to be too clingy in front of our friends, so I had to put up with this for a couple more hours until we could go back home. I mean even if I couldn't be close to her, I still admired her beauty from afar and kept an eye out for her.

As another hour flew by, I felt a little dizzy and somehow managed to forget about Jo completely. We played a couple of drinking games and I was forced to take a few shots and consume alcohol, which made my head hurt like hell. My brain was literally throbbing painfully while my throat was still burning like fire but I loved the feeling it ignited and grabbed another drink to gulp it down straight away until my mouth felt sore.

We decided to take a short break to let the alcohol sink deep into our system before we would eventually continue and as we were talking, my eyes were finally scanning the room for Josephine again but to my despair, she was nowhere to be found which caused my heart to beat out of my rapidly beating chest. I panicked as I jumped up from the couch in a fast motion only to fall back down in an unbalanced attempt to walk through the entire house in order to find and embrace her.

I grabbed my phone with my quivering hands and forced my eyes to stop playing games with me as I rubbed them to have a clear vision before I pressed the call button over and over again but she didn't pick up her damn phone and I was about to lose my shit. Where the hell was she? I was beyond scared that something might have happened to her and couldn't stop blaming myself for her absence.

Even though my brain was sending different signals to my swaying legs, I still managed to stroll through the entire house like a maniac while pushing and shoving peolpe out of my way or grabbing them by their shoulders to keep myself steady. The steps I would climb up so easily when I'm sober brought out the worst in me tonight because it took me quite a long time to walk up the stairs due to my drunken state and I couldn't stop cursing under my own breath.

There were only two places left I hadn't walked into: the bathroom downstairs and the storeroom in the hallway, although I had no idea what she would do in a storeroom. I rushed towards the white bathroom door with a golden handle and pulled it open immediately, only to find a brunette girl who was cleaning her hands with soap and a cigarette in her mouth. "Sorry," I apologized before I shut the door again.

On my way to the storeroom, I called Jo for the hundreth time hopelessly hoping that she would finally answer my call but she didn't. Her phone was either turned off now or it needed to be charged and I promised myself that once I've found her, I'd take her home with me right away. I was going insane and took a deep breath in before I grabbed the silver handle with my shaky fingers and pulled the door wide open with mg eyes shut tightly, praying that she would be inside.

When I re-opened my blodshot eyes, my heart sunk deep into my stomach and I had to grab my chest tightly. There she was, looking straight into my eyes with a horrific facial expression but I felt paralyzed and couldn't seem to move my feet, my hands or anything at all. What broke me completely was the sight in front of me. She wasn't alone and once I managed to figure out who the guy all over her was, I lost it completely.

Andrew.

I clenched my fists until my nails dug deep into my palm and bit onto my bottom lip until I could taste some blood in my mouth as a hot and salty tear rolled down my left cheek. Both of them looked at me like a deer caught in the headlights and without further hesitation, I grabbed Andrew by the collar of his shirt and dragged him out of the small storeroom just to have enough space before my fist came in contact with his jawline.

And suddenly I felt sober again, gaining control of my very own body.

...

author's note:

This is basically the bonus chapter from All Too Well with a few more added scenes because that's how it all started after all, but the next one will be intense *wink, wink* :)

A vote and a comment are much, much appreciated.

thank you.

Chapter 2 - The Fight

T ime will tell

flashback

I couldn't seem to get rid of the disturbing image I had seen a couple of seconds ago and that only caused me to break completely, to get angrier, more furious and more disappointed. It was pure torture and I had a very weird and unknown feeling in the pit of my stomach with a thousand question marks in my head. While Andrew was still laying on the ground, I took a glance to my right to stare at Jo's absent facial expression.

She was clasping her body tightly and just stared at me with doleful eyes before she let her body sink down onto the ground to grab her sleeveless top. I could hear her sobs but decided to focus on Andrew instead because she was only distracting me. The longer I stared at his weak body, the angrier I got, so I dropped to the ground and brought another fist to his defined jaw. "Why would you do this? I thought you were my friend!"

He coughed, spitting some blood on my dark blue shirt. "Hear me out first."

"Hear you out?" I scoffed, grasping him by the hem of his shirt to bring his face closer to mine. "Hear you out? Really? I think I've seen enough, I don't need to hear you out." My hands were literally shaking from all the anger that kept boiling inside of me and I knew for sure that I had to let it out somewhere or perhaps on someone.

I pushed him back to the ground and his head collided with the floor while he moaned in pain. "I can explain everything, Miles." What was he going to explain? He was all over my girlfriend and pretended to be my friend although he was hooking up with her behind my back. I closed my eyes to prevent those damn tears from rolling down because they would make me look weak and vulnerable. My knuckles turned white from clenching my fists and my bottom lip was probably busted open since I couldn't stop biting down on it.

"Why? Just tell me why?" I shouted from my lungs with disappointment lacing on my voice and when I opened my eyes again, I spotted quite a few people surrounding us but I could have cared less. I balled my hands and landed another punch into his stomach just to see him wince in pain before I walked over to the girl I loved so deeply, to the girl who broke my heart in the blink of an eye. I was overwhelmed by this situation and had no idea what I should do other than hurt someone and being completely drunk didn't help me at all.

She was still hiding her face behind her small hands and I kneeled down to the ground to glare at her with nothing but disgust. "And how could you do this to me? How long were you cheating on me? How long has this been going on behind my back? Were you ever going to tell me?" I bombared her with questions and although I tried to keep my voice low and steady, I ended up shouting nevertheless.

"Please stop hurting him, Miles. It's... I..." she mumbled, trying to find the right words to cover her faults with but I was not buying any of this.

Instead I felt the urge to vomit because she was making me sick to my stomach. "I am so, so sorry. I wanted to talk to you about it but..."

"You're-" I didn't have the chance to scold her because I felt a pair of strong hands on my shoulders, turning my body around right before a fist connected with my nose and I stumbled backwards as I covered the center of my face seconds before another punch was landed on my right eye. I wiped some blood from my nostrils and exploded with fury as I growled. Due to the alcohol I consumed and my broken heart, I grabbed random objects and threw them around the hall while cursing under my breath. Objects levitated and broke, causing all those people to drop down to the floor and cover their heads with their hands.

"Stop causing a damn scene!" Andrew shouted this time. "You're way too aggressive and obviously out of control. Get yourself together or you'll hurt more people!" My head was still pounding and now my nose was aching but I didn't care. I wanted to feel more physical pain rather than emotional one, so I had to keep hitting Andrew in order for him to defend himself and hit me as well. Burning rage hissed through my entire body and mind, which I could not control. It demanded to be released in the form of violence.

"You are nothing but a pathetic little rat, Andrew. Cheating on your own girlfriend wasn't enough I suppose and now you're trying to steal my girlfriend? I despise you," I said through gritted teeth as I walked closer to him. "You didn't even have the balls to confess what type of pitiful human being you are to an innocent girl. You betrayed her, damn you even betrayed me!"

"Shut up," he mumbled and I could feel a vein pulsing in my forehead. "I know that you're acting this way because of the alcohol in your blood right-"

And without further hesitation, I swung another punch at his left cheekbone. I could tell that this one caught him off-guard and pain erupted from the point of impact. He kept rubbing his swollen cheek before he averted his gaze back to mine. "You really want to fight, don't you? You always want to solve things with your fists. Why don't we settle this by talking instead? You'll regret this."

"There is nothing to talk about you idiot. I want to finish you." That was the breaking point of my patience and I rushed towards the guy that caused my world to come crashing down within mere seconds before I tackled him. I was hurt because in just one night I lost two people I thought I could trust, two people I thought were my friends, two people I would have done anything for. In just one night I lost the only two people who were close to me and that was devastating and cruel.

"Miles!" Toby called out my name from afar, moving closer to me. "What are you doing? Stop this, I don't want to call the police but I guess I have to call an ambulance. You honestly need to control your anger a lot more, stop violating him!"

I rolled my eyes. "It's none of your business. Stay out of this."

"I can't just watch you commit mur-"

"Stay out," I screamed so loud that I could hear my voice echoing through the crowded halls while driving a hand through my hair to mess it up even more. When I turned my head sideways to glance at Josephine one more time, I couldn't find her on her previous spot anymore. I was glad that she was gone because now she couldn't interfere or try to stop me.

"Hit me," Andrew encouraged with a sloppy smile. "Come on, Miles. Hit me. Ruin my face, break my bones, just hit me."

I accepted his offer and reached out to punch him over and over again, shoved my elbows into his ribs and kicked his guts until he fell to the ground. He was wailing and wincing in pain while I shook my hands to get rid of the aching and tingling feeling on my knuckles. What surprised me the most was the fact that he wasn't fighting back. He didn't even try or put any effort into punching me or defending himself, so I forced him to fight back. "Slap me, punch me, hit me."

His mouth was soaked in blood now and he spit it onto my face to mumble some incoherent words while I wiped the crimson red liquid off of my face. "I think I've hurt you enough already, haven't I?" He was right. Although Andrew was the one looking like a complete mess, I was the one who was truly injured. And while his bruises could heal, mine were scratched deep into my heart and mind.

I felt guilty as my fists continued to hit his face and abdomen but I simply couldn't stop myself. I was outraged. Years of wasted friendship, wasted trust and wasted memories added more fuel to my pain and the more I hit him, the slower my fists collided with his body. My sadness and frustration were replacing my anger until I finally stoppe as I pushed myself away from him.

He was a pacifist, I suddenly remembered. He would never hit me back. I could have knocked him out and he still wouldn't have tried to hit me back after regaining his conscious. I wondered and didn't understand why he decided to land two fists on my face without feeling guilty or apologizing at all but didn't continue when he should have.

"You literally broke his face, dude! Enough is enough, cut this nonsense now." Toby and Ravi grabbed both of my arms to guide me away from Andrew to increase the gap between us while James and Mark were taking care of my newly made enemy who probably passed out. There was blood covering my knuckles and my shirt and for a brief moment I felt like passing out too.

"The show is over, go home now and put your damn phones back inside your pockets." I heard Ashton shout at the people surrounding us under his breath. "I don't want anyone to talk about this on Monday or any other day of the week, got it?"

I exhaled a long breath I didn't even know I was holding as I tried to calm down. My chest was rising and falling in a fast pace and the adrenaline inside of my veins kept rushing up and down, causing me to ball my bruised hands. My face had become rigid and my jaw was clamped tight, so tight that my teeth were grinding against each other.

I jumped up from my position, only to be held back by Toby and Ravi who shook their heads repeatedly. "Don't do it Miles. You've hurt him enough."

I smiled before I laughed straight into Toby's face while jerking away from both of them to walk towards Andrew. He looked like a bloody mess and I wondered whether he was still able to breathe after our little brawl but when I noticed that his chest was still moving after each shallow breath he inhaled, I sighed in relief.

I kneeled down to the ground as I moved closer to his ear. "I know your vulnerability Andrew and if you thought this was painful, then you should prepare yourself for what is about to come. This victory may be yours, but I told you that I'd finish you and I will. I will finish you from deep down inside."

...

author's note:

OH MY GOD. Okay. I hate writing fighting scenes and stuff, so I am very very sorry if this sucked (which it did lol). I can't wait to reveal all those secrets and such, so let the games begin :)

As always, a vote and a commet are much appreciated!

thank you.

Chapter 3 - The Aftermath

- -

Time will tell

flashback

I woke up by a pair of feet kicking my sides lightly and the familiar voice of my father shouting at me. "Wake up, damnit."

My eyes felt beyond heavy and I couldn't seem to have the power in me to open them completely, so I just peeked through one eye before I covered my face with both of my hands and groaned, "What?"

"Why the hell are you sleeping on the stairs? Get up!" My father shouted again which only caused my growing headache to get worse. His voice was unendurable when he raised it, especially during the morning hours so I leaned my head back against the staircase and tried to block it out. "Miles!"

I moaned in pain when I tried to sit up straight because my spine was braced and I had a cramp on the back of my neck. I tried to massage my neck but only winced in pain again when I did the wrong move. "What do you want?" I mumbled without opening my eyes to look at his face due to the soreness in my right eye.

"I demand answers, son. When did you come home and why did you sleep on the damn staircase?" he questioned while tapping his feet against the wooden floor. When I peeped at him through my eyelashes, I noticed that he was in a bad mood and that upset me even more. He was about to let his anger out on me like he always does instead of solving his problems with whoever created them in the first place. "Is that... Is that human blood on your shirt?"

I sighed out loud while pulling my body up from its position to stand right in front of him but every single move added more pain to my already hurting body and muscles. "I got cheated on and I had a fight because of that."

"A fight? What the... How many more times do I need to tell you to stop this nonsense? When will you finally get rid of your childish behavior?!" he screamed, folding his arms in front of his chest while the vein on his neck popped out. This time my mother came rushing towards the staircase with confusion written all over her pale face. Great, she's the least person I needed to see right now.

"It is none of your business!" I shouted right back. "And yes this is human blood on my shirt because I was drunk and angry and I let my anger out on a person who deserved it." Once I finished my sentence, I pulled the dirty shirt over my head and threw it at his face, earning a strong slap from him afterwards.

I bit down onto my already bruised bottom lip and winced in agony as I shut my eyes tightly. "Stop being so disrespectful towards me. How many more times do I need to teach you to be respectful towards your parents, huh? Go look at yourself in the mirror, just look at you. Look at your knuckles, your lips, your swollen right eye. When will this stop? When will you finally grow up? And then you have the audacity to come here complaining that some girl cheated on you. If you keep acting this way, even your next girlfriend will cheat on you - why? Because women want men by their sides, not kids."

I swallowed the deep lump in my throat before I turned around to walk into my room but he didn't let me go. He had a tight grip on my elbow but my body felt numb so it didn't even bother me at all. "Not finished yet?"

"I am sick of you, Miles. You either learn to behave or you leave. Understood? And now go lock yourself into your room and don't come downstairs until you've thought about your actions and the concequences of your actions," he demanded as he took one step closer to me with a condescending look in his brown eyes. "Perhaps take a shower before you do."

After he finally dismissed me, I jerked away from his grip and rushed up the stairs but stopped for a brief moment when I had to walk past my mother. I looked her in the eyes and saw nothing but disgust and disappointment in them - like always. She just shook her head at me while pushing her eyebrows together before she disappeared downstairs. They loved to punish me, blame me, make me feel worthless and I couldn't and didn't want to deal with that anymore. I may be a bad son, but they are even worse parents.

...

I locked myself in the bathroom and turned the shower faucet on to release some hot water and get rid of the silence inbetween these four walls. Not even ten minutes later, the room was filled with steam and I was glad that I couldn't see my reflection staring back at me in the mirror due to my current state of mind and outward appearance. I stripped my pants and underwear down quickly before I walked towards the shower cabin to block out the world once I stepped inside.

The water burned my entire body and I closed my eyes as the heat soaked deep into my skin and massaged the tensed muscles along my spine. I drove both of my hands through my wet hair and leaned my head against the white wall opposite me while moaning in satisfaction and relief. It felt as if the water had the ability to vanish off the burden on my back for as long as I stayed in the shower and I didn't want to step out of it ever again. The last twenty-four hours had been wild and I didn't even get a chance to think about everything that happened properly and with a sober mind and this place was the best place to rewind those horrendous twenty-four hours..

Hot steam was rising to my aching face and I nearly cried out in pain because my lower lip felt sore. My body was in aching pain, my mind was in shreds and my heart was broken into small pieces, yet I didn't have enough time to realize that. I could feel the knife Jo stabbed into my chest and how it kept bleeding after each motion just like I could feel the stab I received from Andrew, so I stopped moving completely and sat down onto the ceramic floor beneath me while burning water kept rushing down my spine.

How was I ever going to get that sight out of my head? The images were floating in my mind like photographs and I just couldn't find a reasonable explanation for what I had seen. "How and why?" I whispered to myself as water dripped down my hair and along my jawline. I knew I had to talk to her but I had no idea how. I had no idea whether I could look into her mesmerizing eyes without being put under her spell again. She had such a strong impact on my life and I was too attached to her to let her go although I had to.

I honestly felt like asking the water to dissolve all my thoughts and memories that revolved around- and reminded me of Josephine. I shielded my eyes to stare at my burning skin which turned red from the hot temperature of the water and released a loud sigh. I wanted to shout, scream, vent, release my anger, break things, punsh the cold bathroom floor until my knuckles bleed again, turn the water even hotter to burn in physical pain but I didn't have it in me. I just wanted to suffocate with my thoughts.

I was weakened, broken, damaged, hurt, in pain and miserable. My eyes became glassy and after I blinked, my salty tears mixed with the water pouring down from the showerhead above me as I started to cry like a stupid little boy. I bit down onto my tongue and inner cheeks in an attempt to hide any noise to escape from my mouth but I failed. Two people I trusted betrayed me in the worst way possible, hurt me in the most cruel way and humiliated me by hooking up behind my back.

I wanted to drown, wanted to disappear, wanted to sink deep into the ground and never come back. I wanted to get rid of everything she and I had, every moment, every kiss, every touch, every midnight talk, simply every memory. She was the one who cheated on me and stepped on my dignity, yet I still couldn't stop blaming myself for what happened. Was it really my fault? Could I have prevented it?

What about Andrew though? What was his reason? Why did he feel the need to hurt me like that, betray me like that, play me like that? I always tried to be a good friend to him whenever he needed me. I would have moved mountains just for him to be happy with his girlfriend - I would have done anything for him because he would have done the same and even more for me if I wanted him to. At least I thought he would.

I felt so numb as I stared at the showe wall. I had no idea whether I was still alive and if I was, I wondered how my broken pieces would get unbroken again, how the images in front of my eyes would vanish, how I was supposed to find hope in the hopeless. I cried until I couldn't anymore.

I cried until my tears ran out and my voice felt sore. I may be breathing, but I was surely dead inside.

"Miles?" I heard my father call out my name after the third loud knock on the door I tried to ignore. "It's been four hours, open up the door."

I gulped once I turned the faucet off because I was confronted with reality again, "Give me five more minutes."

"Hurry up."

Just because I was broken, it didn't mean I had to stay broken. I may be in hell right now and it doesn't seem like I could escape or bloom from my ashes anytime soon, but I knew I how to drag Andrew and Josephine down here with me.

-

author's note:

Just in case some of you are wondering, there are not many flashback chapters left! (I mean there will still be flashback chapters throughout the story, but I just thought I'd let you know that this story won't contain flashbacks only.)

A vote and a comment of your thoughts is very much appreciated! Thank you for your continuous support towards All Too Well and Time Will Tell, it truly means the entire world to me. You guys are truly the best.

I love you.

Chapter 4 - The Lie

Time will tell

flashback

"Aren't you going to talk? You've been sitting here staring at me for the past thirty minutes and I honestly don't know what to do," she mumbled, "or what to say."

I continued to stare at her with my eyebrows pushed together and my lips forming a straight line while my eyes were narrowed down on her. Just like her, I had no idea what I was supposed to say. I came here to talk, to confront her with what I had seen, to argue and to let her know how deeply hurt I was, but once I stepped inside her familiar room, my mind went blank. "Why?"

"Why w—" she cut herself off before she could finish her sentence and avoided to look into my eyes or my direction at all. She was sitting at the other end of the room while I decided to sit on her windowsill and the distance between us was still too small for me. "I never wanted this but it just happened-"

"Things like that don't 'just' happen, damnit!" I shouted so loud that her eyes nearly popped out of their socket and she had to swallow hard. "I am not here to listen to anything you say other than the damn reason why you had to cheat on me, hook up with one of my closest friends and leave me here like a stupid fool, Josephine. Tell me the reason and you'll never have to see this face again."

"How should I explain something to you when I don't even know how it happened myself? I understand that you're hurt but that doesn't mean that we can't try it again, does it? I love you, Miles and I won't ever stop loving you," she said with a quivering voice and I felt the urge to laugh. "I can't and don't want to lose you."

"You're pathetic. Everything that comes out of your mouth is pathetic. I trusted you, I loved you with everything I am — you were my first love and you're not even aware of the damage you caused. Don't you understand that I can't look into your eyes without feeling disgusted by you?" I was bad at putting my thoughts into words whenever I was angry, but I was still trying my best to make her understand that there would be no 'us' from now on.

"Miles," she cried rushing towards my direction before she kneeled down in front of me and grabbed my hands in hers. "It wasn't my fault, I swear! I didn't want to tell you at first, but I can't bear to lose you forever."

I jerked away from her grip and exhaled out loud. "Explain."

She wiped her tears away and nodded repeatedly. "All of what happened is Andrew's fault. I think he was jealous of our relationship ever since you told him about it because his own relationship was miserable. I- I didn't know what to do whenever he asked me for advice and then it all started somehow."

"Wait what?" I shook my head as I shut my eyes tightly. "What does that mean? Did you two meet each other behind my back? Why didn't you tell me about this while it happened?" So she basically confirmed that both of them made a fool out of me for months and I wondered when she would have told me if I didn't find it out myself.

"He didn't want me to tell you. I think he truly loved that girl —the one he dated—but at the same time I had a feeling that he loved me too and he just asked me for all those advices to be close to me... I don't know it's very complicated. I was scared and anxious." She played with her thumbs as she mumbled those words while I was trying to process each word that came out of her mouth.

"And how exactly is all of this Andrew's fault?" I asked harshly. "You could have stopped meeting him, could have stopped helping him, could have told him to leave you alone. This is pathetic, spare me your lies I'm going." I pushed her away from me as gently as I could before I tried to walk past her but she was faster and locked the door to prevent me from walking out.

"I tried to stay away from him but he didn't let me. He is sick, Miles. This was his plan all along: to ruin our relationship just like he ruined his own. He didn't want to see you happy, see you smile, see you by my side. The night you saw us he forced me to kiss him and do...you know," she whispered the last part and now I was more confused than ever. None of what she said seemed to make any sense to me and I had no idea what to believe or what to do.

"Are you lying?"

"No, no I swear I am saying the truth! I am sure that Andrew has a sick obsession with me and he did it all on purpose. Miles please don't leave me." She wrapped her hands around my neck and forced me to pull her into a hug but I jerked away again. "Don't go." I couldn't recognize this girl and at that very moment I didn't even know whether I had ever truly known her or the person she pretended to be. She continued to cry in front of me while I continued to stare at her with my eyes focused on her own. Was this the same innocent girl I fell in love with two years ago?

I'd lie if I said I didn't feel the urge to cry too. I was so damn broken and the fact that I lost a lover and a best friend in one plus another close friend added more pain to my open wound and it was very hard to act like the tough boy I apparently was not. What if she was saying the truth though? I mean Andrew did ask a lot of questions about Jo and I most of the time —questions such as 'Is everything alright between you two?', 'How is Jo doing?', 'Did she tell you what's on her mind?', 'Did you talk to Jo today?' and so on.

Did he really have a sick obsession with her? And why didn't she tell me earlier about this? It was too late now. I was way too focused on revenge, way too focused to hurt Andrew with the same weapon he hurt me with, way too focused to see him hurt like me. "I don't want to see you for now. I want you to leave me alone until I decide to contact you again, okay? I need some space, some time to think about everything that happened."

"Miles—"

"No." I took a step back and held both of my hands out to keep her away from me. "I want you to respect that in order for me to forget all of this." I obviously couldn't get over what happened because those dirty scenes were engraved deep in my brain and whenever I closed my eyes I was reminded by it.

And then I finally walked out of her room and thought about a perfect way to get revenge on both Andrew and Josephine to make them suffer the way I suffered, to make them feel miserable, to ruin their lives like they ruined mine.

Little did I know that I'd ruin an innocent life instead.

—

author's note:

Oooooooooooooookay we obviously know that Josephine is lying here to save herself and put all the blame on Andrew. We all know what happens next, don't we? Ugh. I had the worst writers-block for the past couple of weeks and that's why it took me ages to write and update this, so I am truly sorry if this chapter sucked because if it did, just tell me and I'll make sure to re-write it!!

The next chapter will be a chapter written in present tense and I honestly can't wait to write it oh my. A vote and a comment are much, MUCH appreciated loves.

Thank you.

Chapter 5 – Year I: The Suffering

T ime will tell

—

Being stuck in the past instead of living in the now was one of the things I was very good at lately —and there weren't a lot of things I was good at. For example, I was good at blaming myself, damaging myself, torturing myself and most importantly: hating myself. I was truly and utterly hating the person I was and due to all the stuff that happened in the past, I wasn't able to forgive myself in order to continue my life the way I probably should. I was doomed — doomed to failure, doomed to suffer, doomed to be unhappy for the rest of my pathetic life.

It has been a whole damn year, 12 months, 52 weeks, 365 days and I still couldn't move on or make peace with my past and I had a strong feeling that I would feel this way for the next thirty years and even further. I never thought that I could hate a person as much as I was currently hating myself. If only I could go back in time and change myself and everything that happened, I would within a heartbeat.

I was stupid, so stupid. I was blinded by another person's mistakes, another person's sins, another person's stupidity and instead of being the stronger, more mature person, I proved to be even dumber. I didn't realize the damage I caused while it happened, but I had enough time to rewind those years every minute of the day now and the more I thought about it, the more the anger towards my own self kept rising. How could I have been such a despicable person?

I was an innocent soul when my significant other turned out to be a demon, a devil in disguise, my worst nightmare and she poisoned me with her venom, she introduced me to hell, turned my life upside down. I could never put into words how much she actually hurt me and I would never wish that type of pain upon anyone — emotional pain, the worst type of pain there was. Being stabbed and played by a person you thought you had a future with was harsh and unhuman, it was ruthless and truly heartbreaking... but for some very stupid reason, I was the one who hurt another person, another innocent, pure and sweet soul the way the devil hurt me and that broke me from the inside out.

Once I realized the actual damage I had caused, I felt nothing but disgust and hatred towards the person who stared back at me whenever I looked into a mirror. After that day, I promised myself to never hurt another person ever again and therefore, I decided to stay out of people's lives. I decided to avoid meeting new people, avoid making new friends, avoid females and relationships at all costs. I was a monster who spread nothing but negativity and unhappiness around, a monster who was the reason behind the scars on an innocent girls body who did nothing but love this evil monster even though he gave her millions of reasons not to.

She didn't see the monster in me, no. She only saw the person she wanted me to be, the person I pretended to be, the person she fell deeply in love with. Even after everything I had put her through, she still believed that we had a future and I always wondered how different our lives would have been if I had admitted how much I actually loved her when we still had a chance to work things out. I wondered how much greater our lives would have been if I had been honest towards her from the very beginning.

I ruined it. I ruined everything. I ruined her, I ruined myself, I ruined her life, I ruined my life, I ruined her future, I ruined my future, I ruined her dreams, her hopes, her aspirations, her view on love. I ruined everything we could have had, everything we could have been, everything we could have become, simply everything.

I put her through hell over and over again and she still didn't stop loving me. She truly loved me and I wondered how that was possible. She loved me and I let her go. She loved me and I treated her like a piece of trash instead of treating her the way she deserved to be treated. She loved me and I simply didn't cherish her. She was the most beautiful flower in my garden and I forgot to water her, forgot to take care of her, and most importantly: forgot to love her.

But trust me Rose, if we loved again, I swear I'd love you right.

"You've been stuck on that same page for an hour now, are you alright?" my roommate Baldwin chimed in to pull me out of my thoughts and I put the book in my hands aside to drink some water because my throat felt dry. Although I told him that I didn't want to be anything other than his roommate during College several times, he always insisted to be my friend as well and so I unwillingly let him call me his friend. "We've been sharing this dorm for a year now and you always drift into some deep thoughts... and I just wanted to ask whether you'd like to talk?"

I rolled my eyes while gulping the water down and once I was done, I turned around to face him again. Baldwin was a great guy, no doubt about that but I didn't want to be close to anyone, I didn't want to share my life and my past with anyone because once he'd find out what kind of asshole I am, he'd only leave me as well. "I'm doing great, amazing even, fan-freaking-tastic, don't worry."

He chuckled, "Is it because of Stephanie?"

"Steph— what? I don't give a shit about Stephanie, who the hell is Stephanie?" I asked him before I sat down onto my squeaky bed. As I said, I didn't care about girls or having the time of my life while at College because I didn't deserve to be happy and therefore I avoided to be happy. I loved to torture myself and this was just another perfect way to do so. I needed to suffer, feel miserable, needed to put myself into a different state of pain by abandoning myself from everyone.

"I guess you're still a sociopath, Miles." He began to eat the tuna sandwich he bought yesterday as he shrugged, which only caused me to sigh out loud. A year later and I still had no idea why he labeled me as a so called 'Sociopath'. "I bet you're wondering why I called you one again, don't you?"

I looked up at him and nodded before I faced the wall next to me. "I am not a sociopath," I mumbled, rubbing my sleepy eyes.

"I am studying psychology and trust me when I tell you that you are one. Look," he said, putting his sandwich aside to focus on me intensely. "I am not saying this to hurt you in any way but we need to work on your lack of socialization. And that's not even the reason why I say that you're a sociopath, mate. In his work 'The Psychopath Inside', sir James Fallon breaks down the definition of a sociopath into four categories and I'd say that you belong into category one and four in some way."

I shrugged without actually knowing what he was talking about but I wanted him to stop interacting with me, so that I could drift back into some deep thoughts. "Call me whatever you want to call me, I don't care."

"I'm just trying to help you and figure you out, don't get me wrong. I am trying to understand why you are the way you... are. There must be a reason for your behaviours and—"

"Don't," I cut in with a slight bit of anger lacing on my voice now. "Just don't, Baldwin. I told you that I didn't need a friend or a lover or whatever, so why don't you just leave me alone? You'd do both of us a favour if you did."

"You attract a lot of girls—"

"I don't freaking want to!" I shouted this time, "I don't want to attract a single girl, don't you see it? Look at me, I look like a mess. I don't eat regularly, don't shower as much as I used to, don't shave my damn beard, don't get a new haircut every week, don't work out, don't sleep, probably smell like garbage and you're here telling me that I attract girls? What else do I need to do to keep people away from me? I don't understand." My heart was beating rapidly against my chest and I could feel some hot tears in the corners of my eyes but I didn't want to cry in front of him, didn't want him to see me in such a vulnerable state.

"Why are you torturing yourself like this?" he whispered, taking his glasses off to narrow his eyes at me. "I'd be happy if a girl even looked at me and you're avoiding them."

I bit down onto my bottom lip until I couldn't feel anything but taste the blood in my mouth instead as I covered my face with both of my hands. "I am paying for my sins. As cliché as it may sound, I don't date anymore. I don't ever want to interact with females again, don't ever want them to get close to me, don't ever want them love me."

"I am honestly trying my best to understand you right now, but I can't. This is the longest we have ever talked ever since we met and I am currently trying to let that sink in, man." He rubbed his brown eyes before he put his glasses back on. "What makes you feel and think this way?"

And that was my cue to remain silent again. I wanted to walk out of this dormroom and lock myself inside the janitor's room to cry my entire heart and soul out like I've been used to. I wanted to be left alone with my mistakes, my past, my demons, my sins...just everything. "Enough for today."

I wrapped myself around my blanket and pretended to sleep in order for him to finally stop talking to me. He knew damn well that I wouldn't sleep though and that's why he tapped my shoulder lightly. "Here, read it."

"What is this?"

"Please just read it," he demanded nicely and I did as I was told. "Number one and four only."

Four Categories You Should Consider To Define A Sociopath:

Interpersonal: This category involves interaction with other people. In this area, someone who is a sociopath is superficial and incapable of deep, meaningful relationships and connections. It might seem at first that this person is very attached and caring, but that's just an act. A sociopath is antisocial; he (or sometimes she) is capable of lies and deception in order to get his or her way, but he cares nothing about forming real friendships and partnerships.

Antisocial: The definition of a sociopath centers on this concept. This person stands apart from the rest of society; he exists for himself and only for himself. He cares nothing for the norms, rules, and laws of society. Accordingly, a sociopath has a history of juvenile delinquency and likely has a criminal record in adulthood.

When I was done reading those two definitions, I placed his smartphone back onto his drawer and wrapped myself around my blanket again to face the white wall next to my bed instead of his presence opposite me. Maybe he was right. Maybe I had turned into a sociopath. Maybe I was destined to live my life this way.

And maybe this was just the perfect way for me to suffer.

—

author's note:

If you guys remember the 'The Hurting; The Healing; The Loving' chapters from All Too Well, then congrats because there will be three 'The...'-type of chapters for Miles too (just for you to compare how Rose and Miles coped with their past!)

I hope you enjoyed this chapter! And if you did, please don't forget to vote and to comment your thoughts down below :)

Much, much love!

Thank you.

Chapter 6: Year II: The Hurting

T ime will tell

I was walking along the ocean shore for the past four hours until I decided to sit down and rest because my feet hurt. Although it was past midnight, the moon provided me with enough light and I grabbed a couple of sea shells next to me to admire their beauty. The sound of seagulls and the waves flooding the shore filled my ears with serenity around this time and I enjoyed every second of it.

I turned my head sideways to see how much I had walked since my foot prints were still visible on the wet sand but soon, the waves that kept rolling back and forth from the shore erased them; and like all those past months before, I wished that it would erase me too. I wished that the water would clung at my feet and pull me deep into the ocean, so deep that I wouldn't ever be able to get out again and drown in my misery.

The beach was the right place to reflect on my life — something I did nearly every single minute of the day — because I felt isolated from the rest of the world. It was just me and the ocean; just me and the waves crashing against the shore, the cliffs and my crossed legs in white foam spray every now and then. As always I closed my eyes to listen to the beautiful lullaby of the ocean and smiled to myself for a brief moment as the scent of the water filled my nostrils.

The beach was also the perfect place to drown in my feelings, my emotions, my past, my mistakes, my pain and my thoughts. Just a year ago I was screaming and crying and shouting my lungs out at the ocean to help me, to save me, to rescue me, but now I was sitting here in silence with my bare feet touching the sand and my dark thoughts taking over me. This silence was suffocating me, torturing me, adding more pain to my open wound and I simply hated it.

Whenever I was sitting here at around midnight, I couldn't stop myself from reminiscing about the times Rose and I spent here — well, not exactly here but at the beach in our hometown. I couldn't stop myself from thinking about our first kiss, our first intimate moment, our first adventure. I kept rewinding and replaying those moments and memories in my brain over and over again until they turned into some kind of torture. I was hopelessly hoping to turn back time in order to re-live everything we had for one more time and make it right.

I remembered how my heart nearly dropped out of my chest once those big ruby lips connected with mine for the first time. My brain forgot how to function properly and some of those dead butterflies in my stomach came back to life because of a simple kiss we shared. She revived me but in return, I killed her. While she gave me thousands of reasons to live, to smile and to love again, I gave her a million reasons to hurt herself, to hate her life and to turn her back towards love. Everything that happened was my fault and that was eating me alive day in, day out.

I stared at my wrist and caressed my thumb over the spot of the rose tattoo I had gotten recently. At first I planned to get her name tattooed on my achilles heel since she was my weakness, someone who made me feel vulnerable in every way and every state, but I changed my mind right before the tattoo artist had the chance to pierce through my skin. Why? Because I was the reason she had those permanent scars on her wrists and I wanted to be reminded by that whenever I stared at my own wrist.

I wanted to be reminded by the damage I had caused. I wanted to be reminded of my stupidity, my past that was still part of my present and future, but most importantly: I wanted to be reminded by a person who I loved so deeply and who truly loved me back even though I didn't deserve it. I wanted to be reminded by the fact that I chose a pathetic, miserable and lonely life instead of a life filled with joy, love and happiness. I knew that I chose the wrong path but I wasn't surprised because my life was full of wrong choices and wrong people.

My attention was drawn to my phone once it started to vibrate in my jean pocket and I rolled my eyes the second I read the caller ID - Baldwin. "What?" I picked up the phone rather annoyed although he must be used to my attitude already. I didn't like to admit it, but I actually liked Baldwin a lot. He was a shy guy with a very low self-esteem because he was bullied throughout his entire life and never received the love he deserved. Yet he still tried to enjoy his life as long as it lasted and that was powerful to me.

"Uh... hi Miles," he yawned before he remained silent for a couple of seconds. "Are you going to be back soon?"

"Why?" I asked, rubbing my temples in order to get rid of my own tiredness that seemed to take over me. The moon was shining at its brightest tonight and I really loved that because it kept the darkness from consuming me completely.

"Because I want to lock the door from the inside and go to sleep and you know how deep I sleep so I won't hear it when you knock on the door a—"

"Why?" I asked again but with a hint of curiosity lacing on my voice this time. We usually don't lock our room so I wondered why he wanted to lock it tonight.

"David and Michael informed me that a couple of older college guys would be invading rooms at around midnight and turn those rooms into a mess, steal stuff and apply makeup onto our faces... I don't want that to happen to me, or perhaps to us," he explained and I couldn't stop myself from chuckling into the speaker while listening to him talk.

"If any of them even dare to apply foundation to my face, or perhaps to ours," I mocked him in the kindest way possible, "I'll print my knuckles onto their cheeks don't worry. Go to sleep now because I might not even come back tonight Baldwin, so good night and sleep tight." I turned my phone off after hanging up on him and placed it onto the wet sand next to me.

I always wanted to reach out to Rose; send her a message and ask her how she's doing, what she's up to, where she is living or staying right now, whether she attended college or not and so on. I had billions of questions for her but I couldn't gather enough courage to make the first move. I was too scared, too anxious and too frightened that she might reject me — which she obviously would and I honestly couldn't blame her.

All I wanted was for her to be happy. I wanted her to be truly and genuinely happy. I wanted her to smile the way she used to before I destroyed her — the smile where her eyes became so small and her white teeth came to view just like her right dimple. I wanted her to laugh like there was no tomorrow, laugh so loud until her voice changes from normal to squeaky, laugh so hard that she had no choice but to squeeze her eyes shut tightly because of all the joy taking over her. I wanted her heart to be filled with love, positive energy and happiness in order for her to continue radiating nothing but the beauty within her soul to the people around her.

But the most important task I had to do was to apologize. An apology couldn't turn back time or erase those years out of our minds, but it could help me heal. I wanted her to know that I was truly sorry for what I had put her through. I needed her to know that I was a miserable wreck without her, that I lost the source of light in my life, that I lost the joy of living, the joy of smiling, of laughing, of sleeping, of thinking, of eating, of everything. Maybe, just maybe, she'd feel better once she found out that I was on the verge of giving up.

That's why I was writing — or at least trying to write — a letter for her. I didn't want to share my thoughts with anyone but her and since I couldn't gather enough strength and courage to call or message her and since I had no idea where in the world she was staying at, I decided to do it oldschool. Rose deserved an apology, she deserved to know how broken I was, how damn hurt I was and how bad my life was currently going. She was the color of my life and when she left, it turned black and white. Now the color black was slowly dominating the picture and I had no idea how long I could keep up with it until all white bits would be vanished.

Sometimes this life doesn't treat us right and I don't know what to do but I know it's better with you, Rose.

—

author's note:

Wheew added a bit of Jesse McCartney into this chapter :) no but all jokes aside, I think I have lost the 'magic' of writing. I am never pleased with the outcome of my chapters and I can just repeat myself and tell you that I am truly sorry for it! I am working on getting better though.

A vote and a comment would be much, much appreciated.

PS I am sorry for any typos or sentences that don't make sense!

thank you, I love you.

Chapter 7: Year III: The Healing

T ime will tell

"Miles!" Baldwin shouted, closing the door with his right foot before he came rushing towards me with excitement and happiness written all over his pale face. "You won't believe what I got right here."

I stared at whatever he was holding in his hands and let out a loud breath. "Well, I guess you're going to tell me."

He began to jump up and down like a little kid who just got some ice cream for free and for some odd reason, it made me smile. "Okay- wait, uhm... prepare yourself."

"I am prepared," I remarked as I scratched my elbow. "Don't make such a big—"

"You're going to see Green Day."

My mouth fell wide open and I forgot how to breathe out of a sudden. His words kept echoing through my mind like a broken casette player and

I balled my fists to prevent my arms from shaking like crazy. He had got to be kidding me. I was overwhelmed and shocked in a good way because there was this certain feeling in my heart that made it beat twice as fast. "Wha- what?"

"Throughout these past years I managed to figure out how much you love Green Day and how much their music means to you but since you've abandoned yourself from the outter world, I thought I'd do you a favor and help a friend out. You have no idea how hard it was to get these," he explained with a heart-warming smile. "Plus they're front row!"

Without further hesitation, I pulled him close to my chest to give him a hug that was long overdue. It felt odd to break my shells but it was worth it. Baldwin has been nothing but the best person on earth and he deserved to have a true friend and since he considered me his 'bestest' mate, I could proudly say that he was my 'bestest' mate either. "Thank you."

"Are you alright, Miles? Why, what when and how—"

"Thank you so much," I repeated as he pulled away to hand me those tickets I had been waiting for all my life. "You bought two tickets but said that only I was seeing Green Day instead of we."

"Yes, I bought two for you and another person of your choice. You know...a person who you'd like to accompany you." When he said that, I hit him on his shoulder playfully and a smile spread across his face.

"Baldwin, I obviously want you to accompany me," I said whole-heartedly. "All we have to do now is to turn you into a Green Day fan. I have each and every single album and EP, so you know what to do for the next couple of months, right?"

He nodded while he chuckled. "And you need to go get a haircut, rest well and perhaps take a long shower."

"Deal," I laughed as I held my hand out for him to shake which he gladly accepted. With a gesture like this, he really managed to pull me out of my misery for a brief moment. I mean I was still stuck in the hole I buried myself in, but I had a friend who was desperately trying to get me out of it because I couldn't do it on my own. I appreciated him more than I would ever confess but was really happy that I had him around and I was pretty sure that he was aware of that.

"Miles?" Baldwin broke the silence between us while staring at something on my desk and once I noticed what he was looking at, I grabbed it to hide it behind my back. "What is that?"

"Nothing in particular." I tried to shrug it off although I knew that he wouldn't just drop it but be stubborn and annoy me instead.

"Do I really look like an untrustworthy person to you? I mean I have told you millions of things about me but I literally know nothing about you at all. I always try my best to be a friend to you, even though you keep rejecting me but for the past months we've made such a big step into the right direction and it kind of hurts that you're still not trusting me with anything related to you," he said rather sadly and I rubbed my eyes to get rid of this headache he caused me whenever we were talking about this topic.

"Whether you'd like to believe it or not, I trust you," I replied, folding my arms in front of my chest. "This has nothing to do with trust though. It has something to do with me not wanting to open my own wounds but in order for me to tell you something about myself, I have to rip those damn wounds wide open and let them bleed again."

"If it bleeds, I can help you wrap it with a bandage," he suggested playfully which made me laugh for a split second before my facial expression hardened. I hated to do this, I truly did but at the same time I felt a pressure from inside to finally let it all out and talk to someone about this state of mine.

"It's a letter," I managed to say after a few minutes of silence.

"To whom?" he asked barely above a whisper as he sat down onto his bed opposite mine.

"A girl," I replied briefly while staring at the white envelope in my shaky hands.

"And who is this girl?" he asked again, rubbing both of his hands in a slow pace and I could tell that he was very nervous from the way he talked because he was scared that I would snap at him for being too curious.

"It is a girl I deeply hurt. I... I can't even put into words how bad I hurt her. I turned her life upside down and... I ruined her. I caused her to suffer because I was blinded by revenge," I stopped myself from talking further because I already had tears in my eyes and I knew that I'd start to cry in front of him if I didn't shut up now.

"What did you do though, Miles?"

"Give me a minute," I excused myself to walk into the bathroom instead of facing his painful questions. Once inside, I locked the door and turned the shower faucet on to block the noises that were about to escape from my mouth as I started to cry on the bathroom floor for ten minutes to soothe this aching pain on my chest. I was so sick of feeling this way but I guess that was the price I had to pay for making another human feel this way too.

When I managed to get myself together again, I turned the shower faucet off and washed my face but my eyes still remained red and swollen. "Is everything okay?" Baldwin knocked on the door lightly and I sighed out loud before I faced him by swinging the door open.

"Do you really want to know about the story of us?" I wondered, sitting down onto my bed and grabbing a pillow to put behind my back as I leaned against the white wall.

After a few minutes of him just staring at me with a blank facial expression, he nodded as he took his glasses off. "If you want to tell me, then yes I would love to. I am here to listen, not to judge."

"I fell in love with a girl when I was sixteen. She meant everything to me, you know? She was my support system during a rough time in my life and ever since then I felt connected to her in so many ways. I grew up in a household where the words 'love' and 'affection' were unknown and that was mainly because I wasn't related to my parents at all, but I didn't care because I still considered those people my family." I couldn't stop playing with my hands and the corners of my nails out of anxiety as I tried to tell him the story of how I ruined Rose's life.

"Have you ever met your real parents though?"

"No," I shook my head. "But as I said, I didn't care because those people raised me and I grew up calling them my mother and father. It was not a big deal to me."

"I understand," he whispered, impatiently waiting for me to continue.

"I was craving love and once I found my very own source of happiness, I felt as a whole. I dated my ex girlfriend for a bit longer than a year until she decided to cheat on me with a close friend of mine. And suddenly, the person who made me feel complete, made me feel broken, damaged and worthless. I was angry, furious, completely heartbroken and so disappointed because in one night I lost two people who meant the most to me," I said while driving a hand through my greasy hair. Talking about this whole cheating fiasco didn't even bother me anymore because I couldn't care less about Josephine and Andrew.

Baldwin's eyes grew twice their size before he leaned forward,"How did you find out about it?"

I scoffed, "At a party. My whole world came crashing down right in front of my eyes and that's why I was so fixiated to get my payback. The guy my ex-girlfriend cheated on me with had a girlfriend he truly loved but he was forced to break up with her due to him cheating on her with her best friend."

"What?! So he cheated on his own girlfriend with his girlfriend's best friend and then made your girlfriend cheat on you with her boyfriend's close friend? Did I understand it right?" Baldwin re-adjusted his glasses as if it would help him understand this mess Andrew caused back then.

I nodded, "Exactly. I knew that he still loved his girlfriend, or perhaps ex-girlfriend, so it wasn't really hard for me to think of a plan on how to get my revenge on him and now I'm paying the price for lowering myself down onto their pathetic level."

His facial expression changed from confused to a frown before he asked, "What did you do?"

"I made his ex-girlfriend fall in love with me to see him suffer like I did, but harm set, harm get."

"You didn't love her? How long did it last? Did she ever find out?" he nearly shouted out of excitement and curiousity.

"She was a beautiful and intelligent girl and although I tried to avoid those feelings that were growing in the pit of my stomach whenever we hung out, I realized that I had fallen head over heels in love with her. She was the real reason why I believed in love again, she taught me what love even was in the first place, she showed me what it felt like to be truly loved. But I realized all of this when it was over, when she was gone, when I lost the one real thing I've ever known," I admitted while tugging at my heart. The thought of Rose had such an impact on me and I couldn't stop hating myself more for ruining something so wonderful. "I treated her so badly and kept pushing her away from me because I didn't want to admit that I loved her. I was too scared that she might break my heart too because I couldn't endure it a second time."

He frowned, "Did you ever tell her about your intentions?"

"No, she found out about it on her own. I didn't want to tell her that I only used her for my own benefits because that sounds very cruel, so I tried to create some space between us in order for her to move on and get over me. Turns out she never did. You should've seen the look on her face when she..." I couldn't continue because the look on her face haunted me in my dreams only to remind me of the damage I had caused.

"Ouch," he remarked. "But I understand your narrative, Miles."

"No you don't. You're a good-hearted person with positive thoughts only. You would never even consider hurting another human-being like this. This is messed up, hell I am messed up," I scolded, shielding my eyes from him.

"I disagree because you're not. Mistakes are often the best teachers, don't you think? I mean after all you don't know the value of water before the well runs dry," he tried to defend me. He was right, mistakes were great teachers and I definitely learned my lesson, but how was I supposed to turn back time to make it right this time?

"I broke her heart. She's gone. I manipulated her. She's gone. I didn't value her. She's gone. I used her. She's gone. I-"

"Miles!" he chimed in, "Stop. This attitude and this mindset won't get you far in life. You have tortured yourself for way too long, stop it. I understand that you blame yourself for everything that happened because —I'm sorry to say it—, it was your fault, but you need to move on. You were a hurt teenager back then but now you're a mature and grown man. You admit that you made mistakes and I know that you learned from them, so please don't let your life pass in front of your eyes because of it. What's past is past. Focus on the now, focus on the future!"

And the damn tears were present again. "I'm just...I feel so guilty. I'm responsible for those scars on her wrists—"

"No!" Baldwin cut me off enraged. "How is that your fault? Did you force her to cut herself? She did it to herself. You can't control someone else's thoughts. This is not your fault!"

"I gave her reason to hurt h—"

"Stop, shut up!" he shouted so loud that the vein on his neck popped out for a brief moment and I kept my mouth shut immediately. This was the first —and probably last— time that I had seen this frightening look on his face and for a second I couldn't recognize this person whom I shared a dorm with for the past three years.

"I don't deserve to be happy," I mumbled, wiping my tears away once this nerve-wracking silence in our room helped him to calm down. "I deserve to suffer."

I heard him let out a loud sigh before he walked over to my bed and a few seconds later I felt him sit down next to me. "Whether you believe it or not, everyone deserves to be happy. I was bullied my whole life — from elementary school till middle school till I graduated from high school. I was put into trashcans, was called names, was locked into the restroom, pushed against the lockers and a lot more. Those bullies made me suffer my whole life but guess what?"

"What?" I asked hoarsely while rubbing my eyes.

"A few months after our graduation, I met one of my bullies in a grocery story and I was scared that he might do something to me, but he didn't. He stared at me for an entire minute until he walked over to me and apologized for what he had put me through. He told me that he was feeling miserable because of it and that he couldn't live his life the way he wanted to if I didn't accept his apology, so I did."

"You did?" I questioned in disbelief as I snapped my head up to look at him outraged. "Why would you do that?"

"Because I could tell that he was truly sorry. He invited me over for a drink that same day and basically told me everything that was bothering him ever since we graduated," he explained as he placed his hand on top of my shoulder. "What I'm trying to tell you is that maybe you should contact the girl you hurt and ask her for forgiveness."

—

author's note:

I hope you enjoyed this long chapter! I'm not sure whether I got my magic back, but I'm slowly working towards it, so bear with me.

A vote and a comment are much, much, much appreciated.

PS listen to the song above if you'd like to,

thank you & I love you.

Chapter 8 - Let the games begin

T ime will tell

flashback

"Are you sure you want to join us?" Noel asked for the fifth time as he stared at me with concern in his eyes. "I mean your father would kill you if he found out about any of this I hope you're aware of that. I think you forgot about his threat last week."

"I don't care." I shrugged grabbing the key in his hands to walk towards the car he was about to steal from the guy whose dog he used to dogsit over the summer. "Where is the other car?" I asked, turning around confused.

"Over there," he pointed towards an old garage and I nodded. "We'll meet at the main street and then we'll see who can drive faster."

I chuckled, shaking my head in amusement. "I think we both know the answer to that already."

"Don't be so cocky, Miles. I obviously am the better drive since I am a whole year older than you. I am way more experienced and mature," he spat as he opened the door to the car he had already taken without anyones permission.

We had to drive for about ten minutes until we reached the main road downtown and I didn't have a good feeling about any of this because I had a feeling that the police somehow heard about this illegal car race since a lot of people were present. Besides, it was very noisy and crowded and I kept wondering why they would decide to use the main street for this instead of choosing some rural area.

My phone vibrated in my pockets and I picked it up straight ahead, "Yeah?" When I looked to my left, I spotted Noel grinning at me from his car and I returned his smile.

"We're next," he informed me and I put my thumb up to signalize that I got it.

"You can still forfeit or else you'll be humilated." I could hear his laugh from the other line and joined him while tapping my nails on the steering wheel. Although Noel was an older friend of mine, we stopped hanging out as much as we used to due to some unknown reasons. But now I had to ignite this friendship again in order for me to get closer to his sister Rose.

"I'll humiliate you," he remarked and this time I could hear the loud noise he was releasing from his car because he was stepping on the gas continuously as he was getting ready for the race and I did the same.

"Alright bye-"

I was cut off by sirens that kept coming closer and closer and when I turned the engine off to get out of the car to update myself about the situation, I noticed that everyone was either running or driving away. "Shit," I cursed under my breath while inhaling a long breath in after I ended the phone call. Before I had the chance to get back inside the stolen car, someone grabbed my upper arm and dragged me away from it within an instant.

From the corner of my right eye, I could see that another guy got ahold of Noel as well. "Do you own these cars?" the rather strong man asked.

"Yes," I mumbled under my breath.

"Don't lie to me kid." He let go of me to stare straight into my eyes and I had to gulp.

"No," I answered truthfully this time.

"You're in a lot of trouble."

"Who are you?" I asked, adjusting my shirt.

A small smile curved his lips after he grabbed his wallet to show me what's inside and I scoffed out loud once I saw his ID card; he was a cop.

...

"Are you out of your freaking mind, Miles? Are you stupid? What was going through your head when you made that decision? Why are you like this? Are you never going to grow up? I am sick of this, I am sick of you!" My father shouted only a few inches away from my face and I could feel his spit on some parts of my face.

"I am sorry!" I shouted back although I obviously didn't care but he always had to hear an apology in order to calm down a bit but I guess it didn't work this time.

"No! We got a damn phone call from the police in the middle of the night. We were so worried that something happened to you, only to find out that you were part of an illegal car race? Do you have any idea how dangerous this is? I guess you don't. I am sick of repeating these things to you over and over again." He turned around to loosen his tie and drive both hands through his hair before he looked at me again.

"Come on let's get back inside," my mother tried to calm him as she grabbed his arm with both of her hands but my father jerked away and made his way inside on his own while my mother rushed behind him and so did I.

Once inside, I sat down onto the couch in the living room and took a short glance at Noel who was being scolded by his father as well. I was tired and just wanted to sleep and forget about this night but I had a feeling that I wouldn't.

"We're having a deal, right?" my father said to his. I noticed that Noel's mother was crying while mine just stood there like an emotionless tree and I scoffed because she simply didn't care. "And if this doesn't work, you know what will." He said looking straight at me this time.

Noel's father nodded as he brushed away the sweat on his forehead. "That's the plan."

A couple of seconds later, my attention was drawn somewhere completely else as another voice joined the conversation. "May I ask what's going on?" Her voice came out very low and I was sure that no one even noticed her presence other than me.

"Alright," an officer said loudly once he approached us only to say, "I hope you learned your lessons out of this," before all of them walked out of the house.

My parents stormed off right after the police officers disappeared but I remained right at my spot. I didn't want to leave, at least not yet. I had to wait until they were asleep before I could go back home to avoid another confrontation with them.

Noel left his seat and walked straight out of the living room and when he passed by his sister, I could hear her wince in pain for a brief second.

I let out a loud groan before I decided to follow Noel upstairs and ask whether I could stay the night but stopped right in front of Rose. "You okay?" I asked, biting my bottom lip.

Instead of receiving an answer, she just nodded and I could literally feel the nervosity she was radiating from her body so I smiled until she said, "I am."

"Miles!" I heard Mrs. Johnson shout from another room and I looked up at the ceiling before I averted my gaze back to the girl standing in front of me.

"I guess I should get going."

She motioned towards the ceiling with her index finger and nodded again. "Uh-I-I think I should get going too."

When I walked up the stairs, I felt her presence very closely behind - so close that she nearly fell down the stairs when we reached the top. "Good night, Rose Johnson." I could see that I caught her off guard for the second time this night but she tried to hold that back. And after she repeated my words, she rushed back into her room and I sucked my bottom lip between my teeth at the sight of her with some red shorts and bunny slippers.

"Miles!" Mrs. Johnson called out my name again and I tried to figure out where her voice was coming from but she approached me on the hallway before I had the chance to. "You're going to stay here."

"I am?" I asked confused.

"Yes, you are. My husband and your father thought it would be best if you stayed here for a few weeks until your parents think of a way to handle this whole situation," she explained, squeezing my shoulder. "You'll be our guest and live with us, I hope that's okay. I mean we know how cruel your father can be sometimes. Don't worry, it'll all get better in time."

I high-fived myself mentally over and over and over again. Jackpot. Staying in the same building as Rose Johnson made this a lot easier for me — easier than I thought it would be. Making her fall out of love with Andrew just to make her fall in love with me instead should now be a child's game, so let the games begin.

—

author's note:

Writers block is the most annoying and the worst thing to ever happen. I hate it. SO much. SO SO much. Thank you for your patience, I am truly sorry for making all of you wait for so damn long. I know this chapter is lame and very boring but I am trying to fill some plot holes along the way of writing this story and I already started working on the next chapter (which will be present tense again), so it should not take me longer than a week (or two) to update the next one!

A vote and a comment are very much appreciated.

Thank you. I love you.

Chapter 9 - Where are you now?

T ime will tell

"So I'll watch your life in pictures like I used to watch you sleep, and I feel you forget me like I used to feel you breathe [...]"

— Last Kiss, Taylor Swift

...

(warning: I'm really bad at doing graphics and such, so I'd just like to apologize beforehand.)

"So, how is it going?" Baldwin asked, taking a seat next to me with a bowl of cereal in his one hand and a bowl full of fruit on the other. "Wait, did you reach—"

"No," I cut him off. "I mean I didn't even try to find her but...I don't know I mean...you know..." I tried to put my thoughts into words but realized I failed completely when I saw his facial expression — which was a mixture of confusion and annoyance.

"If I were you, I'd definitely try my best to reach out to her!" He nudged my ribs while giving me that look.

"You would actually do that?" I wondered, folding my arms in front of my chest.

"Well no, I mean I would do it if I were actually you," he corrected himself while adjusting his glasses. "With your face and stuff..."

I rolled my eyes at him as I squeezed his shoulder lightly. "I'll do it."

"Yes, come on! Are we going to stalk her on Instagram?" he emphasized the word with an italian accent and I couldn't stop myself from laughing out loud.

"First of all, we won't stalk her," I put my index finger up high to make a point. "We will just check out her page and see what she's up to, you know?"

"Sure," he scoffed. "Be honest, how excited are you? Or perhaps how nervous are you? I mean you haven't seen her in so long. On a scale from one to—"

"I'm not nervous," I scoffed this time although I was nervous as hell. My palms were sweating like crazy and my heart was beating out of its socket. I actually thought that I would pass out without even getting the chance to stalk her on social media.

"Sure," he repeated, putting his now empty bowl aside.

I took a deep breath in before I re-downloaded the Instagram app after all these months of being absent on it. I just couldn't bear to see all those happy couples and happy people in general who were trying to show off how great their lives were while I was a miserable wreck. "It's downloading," I informed.

"Hurry up, I really want to see her."

So do I. "Be patient." I tapped my right foot against the wooden floor while taking another deep and long breath in as this weird, tingling feeling in the pit of my stomach appeared again. It was a feeling I haven't felt in so long and that's why it felt so odd.

"Log in, log in, log in!" Baldwin pressed his elbow into my sides while moving too close to me to get a glimpse at my phone screen, which caused me to jerk away.

"Dude, wait a second," I sighed, pushing myself away from him for a brief moment to get a chance to type my username and password correctly.

Once I logged in, I had to wait until my feed was done loading while the app kept notifiying me about all those new features and updates I missed. And within seconds, pictures of my former friends and classmates popped up on my screen, so I scrolled down to see what they've been up to before I'd do what I came here to do.

"Who is that?" Baldwin asked, leaning in again.

"He used to be a good friend of mine," I said, reminiscing all those times Ravi and I spent together as teenagers. I tapped onto his profile and noticed that he looked a lot more mature now. He had a few tattoos on his shoulders and probably worked out five times a week.

I visited some other profiles as well and could literally feel how my self-esteem was being pulled down again. Everyone was living their best life —or at least pretended to. Some were traveling around the globe, others were enjoying college and the rest were either working or still trying to hold on to their past lifestyle which consisted of partying and alcohol only. I was surprised how some of those people I used to greet everyday became so different now.

"This girl is quite beautiful, who is she?" Baldwin pulled me out of my daze as he tried to grab my phone out of my hand but I didn't let him as I tightened my grip around it.

"Who are y—" I pushed my eyebrows together, "oh, that's Jessica. I met her through another friend of mine during sophomore year I think. She looked completely and utterly different then I swear." Jessica was one of those girls you could talk about anything with. We couldn't really be considered as friends, but we had a couple of long conversations on our way home once.

"So beautiful," Baldwin repeated amazed. "Now show me Rose!"

"Okay, okay." My voice turned into a whisper and I honestly felt like dying. I was scared of what I might be confronted with. I was scared that I wasn't ready to see whatever she had been up to. I was scared that she might be living her best life without me or that she might not even miss me. I know that sounds selfish...I mean of course I want her to be happy — I want her to be genuinely happy more than anything —but I want to be part of her happiness, I want to be part of her smile, part of her world again.

"Do you think she might have blocked you? Were you even following her?" his questions drove me nuts and I was close to lock him out of this damn room but I needed his company, I knew I did.

"We never even followed each other in the first place, so I'll have to find her through some mutual friends — which I hope I do. She might not even have Instagram anymore." I gulped, scratching my neck before I gathered some courage to type in Adam's username. I had no idea whether this idea would work, but I prayed that it would.

"I shouldn't be the one to say this, but I'm so nervous, Miles. I am crossing my fingers for you, mate."

I scrolled through Adam's following list until I spotted Andrew's username and within seconds, I was on his profile. Even though I despised this guy with everything I was, the temptation to see what he had been up to was way too strong, so I gave in.

"This dude right here is Andrew. I hope you remember which part of the story he captures because I really don't want to tell you again." I clicked onto a random picture and held my phone out for him to get a good look at the devil himself while biting my nails.

"This? That's hi- wait, hold on." He managed to snatch the device out of my hand this time before he began to pace back and forth. "I wish I had his looks, are you serious?"

"Hey!" I felt offended. "Whose team are you even on?"

"I am sorry, I just got reminded that life is unfair once again," he reached my phone out for me to take and I did after he jumped back onto my bed with a frown.

"Just remember that you're prettier on the inside," I said truthfully, trying to comfort him somehow before I turned my attention back to my task.

"Being prettier on the inside doesn't get me as many followers as him, does it? He has two thousand!" he crossed his arms in front of his chest as he leaned back against the wall and I noticed that he was quite sad now.

"Two freaking thou—" Once I processed what he just said, my eyes trailed to his follower count and my mouth fell wide open. "Oh come on Baldwin, look at all this stuff he posts. He turned into some sort of wanna-be Instagram model...look at this — look at all these teenage girls swooning over him."

"No thanks. I really don't need to be more depressed than I already am right now."

"I guess he's studying...law?" I whispered to myself while continuing to scroll through his page. I noticed that Andrew hadn't changed at all. Just like Ravi, he became more mature but other than that, he was still the same guy I knocked out a few years ago.

I sighed, "I'll leave his page now, I'm about to throw up."

"Thank you," he mumbled, leaning in again.

Compared to his follower count, Andrew was only following about three hundred people and I was sure that his best mate William must be one of them. But I already spotted the person I was looking for without visiting Will's profile and the blood in my veins felt cold. I was probably exaggerating this whole situation, but I had a feeling that I would leave her page heartbroken.

"I found her."

"Tap on her name whenever you feel ready for it." B's voice felt very soothing and I nodded as I shut my eyes tightly. Three and a half years. It's been three and a half years since I had the privilege of laying my eyes on her for the last time. Three and a half years since I broke her. Three and a half years since I caused her world to come tumbling down. My palms became sweatier, my heartbeat became more rapid and my mind was spinning like crazy.

"I hope her profile isn't private," I whispered but exhaled out loud after I clicked on her username by accident since my thumb was shaking. It said 12 posts, 402 followers and 249 following. I smiled lightly because her caption was a simple quote, which said: "If you can't find the light, be the light."

"I'll use the...bathroom." I heard Baldwin's words echo from afar as I drifted into some very deep thoughts. Once I made sure that he was gone,

I tapped onto a picture and scrolled through her page while getting completely and utterly lost in her beauty.

I couldn't stop myself from smiling like a little child as I scrolled through her page. Rose was happy and that was everything that mattered to me. She recovered, she healed, she learned to let go of the past, learned to love herself, accepted who she was and somehow, that was everything. Even though it hurt like hell, I was glad that she let go of me — I was glad that she found the light she was desperately looking for in me.

But still, nothing in the world could have prepared me for what I was about to see. I grabbed ahold of my heart and gave it a tight suqeeze as a few tears came rolling down my cheeks at the sight of the last picture on her profile and all this remorse inside of me. Suddenly, everything came crashing down in front of me and I started to cry. I was relieved but so, so heartbroken at the same time. She found the light she needed to pull her out of the darkness I consumed her with.

The last time I felt my heart being ripped out of my chest like this was when I was seventeen — right after I found out that my girlfriend cheated on me. But this time it felt worse and it hurt a lot more because this time, I was the one to blame. I did this to myself. I didn't lose the best thing in my life, no, I myself let go of it - let go of her. I guess sometimes God takes the good away from us so that we can sit and think about our mistakes and be a bit more appreciative and grateful.

I changed though. I know that I am not the same guy I used to be three years ago. I made mistakes, but I learned from them. They made me suffer, put me in a lot of pain, ripped me apart and weakened me but I conquered. I survived. I didn't give up. I worked on myself to become a better person. I let go of my past to focus on my future but there was one more thing I had to do before I could close that book once and for all: Ask the girl I ruined for forgiveness.

Your name, forever the name on my lips, Rose.

...

author's note:

I truly hope that you got some Instagram vibes lol! But oh well, did the chapter suck? If you think it did, I am sorry. If you think it didn't, then PLEASE don't forget to vote and maybe even leave a comment down below/while reading. I appreciate each and every single one of you, don't forget that.

thank you, i love you.

Chapter 10 - Change

T ime will tell

Please listen to the song above before reading the chapter!!!!

—

Life was very complicated to understand but so easy to live. Life was nothing but a collection of moments. Moments you would cherish forever. Moments you would think about in the future. Moments you would keep in your heart —or perhaps try to keep in your heart— forever. And sometimes, life was a collection of moments you would want to forget about but simply couldn't because those moments were haunting you; they were part of you.

My life wasn't filled with great moments or cherishable memories, in fact, it was filled with countless mistakes. And somehow, those mistakes didn't want to let go of me. I wondered how different my life could have been if I prevented those mistakes every single day. Life could have definitely been better, brighter and joyful instead of being pure hell for me now. I was twenty-two years old but still stuck in my seventeenth year of life. Why? Becuase I was seventeen years old when it happened. I was seventeen years old when the devil reached his hand out for me and I gladly took it. Up to this day, I still hate myself for it, and I probably always will.

"How come you decided to visit us?" My mother was staring at me for the past ten minutes without saying a single word until now. She wasn't showing any emotion and I was really overwhelmed by this situation. I had to admit that it was odd to be back here—back home I mean. These four walls never seemed like home to me and they still didn't make me feel as if I was actually home at all. It was December and I decided to take a few weeks off college to visit my parents and see how they were doing but most importantly: I came here to apologize and ask them for forgiveness.

"I just wanted to...stop by and see if everything was alright." I couldn't look into her eyes. This situation was very awkward for me. The last time I saw my parents was nearly three years ago. My father and I were arguing once again and we couldn't stop shouting at each other until he told me to leave and I gladly took all my belonging and shut the door behind me once and for all. My mother was crying that night because she couldn't bear our fights anymore. She was sick of me. I knew that I wasn't easy to deal with and like every other hurt person, I had my demons too. And sometimes, they got the best of me but I learned to tame them, learned to get rid of them, even learned to make peace with them.

We were sitting in silence for the hundreth time today before she opened her mouth so say something, but no word escaped from her parted lips. I kept playing with my thumbs as I stared at the pictures hanging on the walls and a small smile curved my lips when I spotted a picture of my father and I because they didn't get rid of it. I was about six years old when my father took me to my first NFL game in Philadelphia and up to this day, I still remember how happy I actually was. His best friend Gerald took this picture of us. While my father was holding me on his shoulders, I was smiling with my whole heart and even at this distance, I could see that my two front tooth were missing. I was wearing an oversized

Philadelphia Eagles shirt and suddenly wondered whether my dad still kept it somewhere.

Staring at those photographs brought back a lot of memories and I could feel my eyes burning. Life was so simple back then. It was so different. I was so different.

I inhaled sharply. "How have you been, mom?" I truthfully wanted to know. I wanted her to pull me into her arms, caress my back and tell me that everything would be alright again. I wanted her to go find my old childhood books and read them out to me. I simply wanted to go back in time and avoid meeting the devil.

She put her tea-mug aside and remained silent while avoiding to look into my eyes now. "What do you think, Miles?" The tension in this room could be cut with a knife. I was scared somehow—scared that she might not accept my apology. Scared that she might not forgive me for all the wrong I've done. Scared that she might abandon me forever.

"I'm serio—"

"Your father was missing you like crazy. He kept asking about you, kept wondering where you were staying, kept wondering how you were doing, Miles. Despite to everything you said to him, despite to everything you called him that night, despite to all the pain you put him through, he was still asking about you every day. Despite to how much you actually hurt him with your words, he was still missing you so much." She nearly whispered those words with disgust, but I could feel the hurt in her voice very loud and very clear.

I licked my dry lips wet and rubbed my teary eyes to stop myself from crying out loud. "I am sorry. I am truly sorry. For everything. I am not perfect, neither are you. I know that I made mistakes, damn, mom I am so freaking sorry for literally every single thing I have ever done wrong. I realize that

I have been a bad son and a bad person. I know how much pain I caused you two, but I bet that you have no idea how much pain my heart had to endure, do you? I was literally done with everything. I reached the lowest point in my life when I was nineteen years old and that is freaking scary, mom. I suffered —and I suffered alone. I had no single person I could trust around me, no single person I could talk to, no single person I could open up to. I thought I was strong but I figured out that I am not. I used to lock myself in my dorm room and cry until my eyes ran out of tears."

"An apology won't fix this." Her eyes seemed to be distant and she didn't blink for another couple of minutes. My mother has never been a soft person but I was shocked about her lack of empathy. She was strict and unhappy most of the time. The only person who managed to make her smile at least a slight bit was my father, other than him, no one else had the ability to vanish the everlasting frown on her face.

I closed my eyes. "You don't understand, mom. I am truly sorry for everything I ever put you through. I know that I was very hard to deal with, but I changed. I am all grown up now. And trust me, if I could, I would turn back time immediately. I swear I'd go back in time and change it, but I can't. We have to make peace with the past and focus on our future now. Can we—"

"Miles, stop it please," she cut me off again, shaking her head repeatedly.

"Do you even care about our relationship? I am trying to fix this, damn it!" I didn't want to raise my voice, so I pinched myself while closing my eyes to stay calm.

"What are you trying to fix though? There is nothing to fix anymore, Miles! We got used to this life without you somehow, you should get used to it too. If you managed to survive the past three years without seeing us or hearing our voice, then you can manage to live without us for the next couple of years as well." She was angry now. But I could see the hurt and disappointment in her glassy eyes.

"Do you think it was easy for me? I needed to just distance myself from everyone and everything. I was a rebel. I was a teenager. I was stupid. Look at me now, I changed," I repeated oh so desperately.

She sighed as she looked me deep in the eyes. "Miles,...."

I stopped listening to my mother's words when I spotted my father standing in the door frame with a pack of chestnuts in his right hand. Seeing my father for the first time after all those years made my stomach turn out of anxiety. Although our relationship was very difficult and although we ended up in a fight nearly every day, I realized that I loved this man. I tried to stay focused, but those chestnuts brought back a lot of great memories from my childhood. My father and I used to collect chestnuts from my grandparents garden in the fall and poked toothpicks through them to create animals and other weird things while my grandma spent her whole day baking a pumpkin cake in the kitchen with lots of cinnamon for me and suddenly, it felt as if I was a five year old again.

He didn't move or say a single word, neither did I. From the corner of my eye I could see that my mother was a bit overwhelmed by his arrival and she jumped up from her previous position. "What are you doing here?" Were his first words and I'd lie if I said it didn't hurt because it did. I was expecting a hug, I was expecting him to tell me that he missed me, I was expecting him to be happy to see me.

"I'm here to beg for fogiveness. I'm here to apologize. I'm here to save and change my life."

He scoffed, "really?"

"Yes," I said with a stern voice while nodding my head.

"Do you really expect me to believe this?"

I had to bite onto my bottom lip to stop myself from just shouting loud because this was harder than I thought it would be. "Give me one more chance and I'll prove it to you, dad."

His eyes softened a bit but he was still hiding behind a facade. "Leave."

"What? No!" I was shocked and could feel my heart being ripped apart in two.

"I said leave," he repeated as he closed his eyes. He was pointing towards the exit and I balled my hands into two fists before I took a deep breath in.

"I'm not going anywhere unless you hear me out. There is so much I need to tell you, so much I need to apologize for. Can you please listen to me, dad?" I was on the verge of crying because I was anxious to lose him forever.

"Hear you out? You abandoned us! You were the one who left us behind without one single note. You were the one who hurt us by treating us like trash! You were the one who ruined so many lives, Miles. You always made me feel like a bad father although I always tried to stop you from ruining your own life but guess what. I didn't manage to stop you from ruining not only your own life but other lives too. Do you actually think that I don't know what you did to Rose Johnson?"

Rose Johnson. The name that was tattooed to my heart and soul forever. The name that always reminded me of my problematic past. The name that held a lot of memories. Whenever I heard her name, I couldn't breathe. Something inside of me prevented me from inhaling oxygen and it hurt like hell. Just hearing her name put me in a lot of pain— pain I couldn't endure anymore. I was stuck in a daze and didn't even listen to what my father had to say next.

"Dad stop." He hit me at my weak spot and now I couldn't bare to listen to him talk. My mind was somewhere else now and I just wanted to be left alone. "You don't get it. I am not the same problematic eighteen year old kid anymore. I'm aware of all the chaos I created in the past - that's why I'm here. I want to make everything right this time. I want to start it all over again. I want to prove to you that I have changed. I want to be a good son to you. I want to go collect chestnuts in grandpa's garden and eat grandma's pumpkin cake. I want to watch silly Disney movies with you while eating corn. I want to wear your jersey while watching another NFL game with you. I want to buy a car and drive around the city while blasting old country music and talk about girls with you. I want to built things again with you. I want to go drink some beer at the bar around the block on Sundays while watching football with you. I want to be your best friend again, Dad."

I could see that he was slowly getting rid of his facade and started to show his true face to me. And as I already thought, he looked truly hurt. He had gotten a lot older within those couple of years. He had a lot more wrinkles on his forehead and his eyes were red. He seemed a lot more tired and his hair was a bit more grey on some parts of his head.

"Dad? Please say something." I finally managed to move my body while keeping my eyes locked with his. I couldn't hold back those damn tears any longer as I started to cry like a small little child who didn't want to be left alone in the darkness because he was scared that monsters might be hiding under his bed.

"Miles?" his voice came out very hoarsely and we just stared at each other for a few more seconds until he let go of the chestnuts to pull me into his arms instead. He gave me a tight hug—a hug I desperately needed. "Where have you been, son?" he cried into my shoulder and for the first time in years, I felt loved again. I felt important and missed - I felt special.

"I'm sorry for that night, dad. I shouldn't have said all those cruel things to you, I shouldn't have been so disrespectful towards you, I shouldn't have let my anger out on you. I was such a bad son and I hate myself for it, I hate myself for all the things I ever put you through. I hate myself for ever raising my voice towards you, for making your life so hard by just being in it." My tears were running wild and I secured my arms around him to make sure that he won't leave me. I was freaking anxious that this might be a dream, so I clung tightly to him.

I hid my face in the crook of his neck and continued to bawl my eyes out. It felt great to cry, to let my tears finally escape from my eyes, and it felt even greater to stop pretending to be strong and the though guy when I was weak and scared instead. I needed my parents by my side, especially my father. "Stop thinking about that, son. I missed you, trust me I did." He didn't let go of me yet and I was glad about that. I could have stayed like this forever because I realized that being in his embrace somwhow felt like home. "Come sit down."

(That's exactly how I imagine Miles' father to pull him into his arms!)

—

author's note:

I AM SORRY FOR ANY TYPOS OR SENTENCES THAT DON'T MAKE ANY SENSE.

THANK YOU FOR YOUR PATIENCE. Holy cow. It's been a while, hasn't it? Life is tough and it's hard to get going sometimes.

I love you all.

Chapter 11 - I'm sorry

T ime will tell

"Creative Writing, huh?" my father said rather than asked as he placed the hot cup of camomile tee onto my desk before he took a seat on the edge of my bed. It was completely odd to be back home, and even more to be sitting in my old room filled with countless memories. Everything looked different to me now. Everything reminded me of days I wanted to forget. It didn't look very familiar to me anymore and that's why I didn't really feel welcome within those four walls.

I nodded slowly. "Yes. I kind of realized that I loved writing. It has become my passion but it took me some time to understand that."

"Did you...graduate already?" I could hear and see how broken he was. He obviously wanted to be standing right by my side when I graduate and cheer me on while I accept my diploma but due to me being an awful son to him, he thinks he missed the most important day of my life although he didn't since I haven't graduated yet.

"Don't worry, I haven't graduated yet dad. But I want you to be right there in the crowd when it happens. I want you to take pictures, cheer my name, but most importantly, I want to see the huge smile on your face when I walk up the stairs to get what I'm working for right now. I want to see how proud your are." I admitted truthfully before I sat up straight to adjust my hoodie.

He felt relieved as he closed his eyes for a brief moment. "We'll be right there. I wouldn't miss it for anything in the world, Miles."

"Dad?" I asked while taking a small sip from my tea. When I nearly burned my tongue from the hot impact, I put the glass aside again to let it cool down for a while.

"Yeah?" he looked up at me which caused me to smile like a little child. I had no idea when I was as happy as I was right now, but I knew that it must have been a couple of years because I had to get used to this unfamiliar feeling again since I wasn't used to it anymore.

"Thank you for accepting my apology. I don't know what I would have done if you—"

"Let's not talk about it, Miles. How could I not forgive you? You're my son. You may not be my own flesh and blood, but to me, you're even more than that. You're my life, my everything, my very own heart. Don't ever forget how much you actually mean to us. Your mother is still quite angry at you, but just give her some more time and she'll eventually let go of her ego and tell you how much she truly loves you, alright?" he squeezed my leg and I nodded while biting my bottom lip.

"I understand. I'm glad that you both exist. I'm grateful for you both. I just want to let you know that, dad. I'm eternally thankful for everything you both have ever done for me." I smiled to myself after finishing my sentence because I could really feel the change within me. Years ago, I would have never said those words out loud but now I did. I managed to get rid of my bad-boy facade and finally managed to talk like a grown-up.

There was a long silence between us until my father decided to break it once he managed to find the right words to express himself. "Why did all of this happen to us? Or perhaps to you?"

"What do you mean?" I asked confused. I was caught off-guard although I was aware of what he was referring to. I really tried to avoid this conversation, but I knew that we'd have to talk about this someday and apparently, someday was today.

He turned his body towards my direction completely while staring deep into my eyes. "Your fights, your attitude towards me, your mood swings, all the partys,.. just everything. Why did you turn into some...some sort of monster? I couldn't even recognize you. I was scared that I had lost you forever."

I sighed, taking a deep breath in. "I don't have an explanation for what I have done. I honestly have no idea how to put my thoughts into words, dad. I was just very, very hurt back then but believe me when I tell you that every single time I look back at what I did, I want to punch myself in the face. I want to punch myself because I was so, so stupid, dad. I was very, very stupid. I ruined something beautiful —something that had the chance to bloom. But I didn't let it bloom. Instead, I let it rot."

"Are you talking about your relationship with Rose?" I heard him say and once her name left his lips, my head shot up in pain.

"How... did you know?" I wondered.

A sad smile curved his lips as he pulled his eyebrows together. "The day after you left, I walked into your room to cry because I was very sad about how you ended things with us. I opened your drawer to grab one of your many hoodies and then I spotted something in there."

"What did you find?" My heart was beating like crazy because I didn't know what he was talking about.

"I found a crumpled up piece of paper laying there."

"A crumpled up piece of— oh my God, dad. Did you find the letter?" I jumped up from my bed in anxiety as my eyes grew twice their size. I truly hoped he wasn't talking about the first letter I wrote her back when we were still 'dating' but when he nodded his head, I squinted my eyes before I drove both of my hands through my hair to mess it up.

"And a few days later, her father showed up at our frontdoor and confronted me with all the mess you put his daughter through. I have never been more humiliated and disappointed in my life than I was at that very moment. You broke an innocent soul because you were blinded by revenge, Miles. Even though I was mad at you, I couldn't believe my ears. I couldn't believe what her father told me about you. I was outraged," he told me while rubbing his sleepy eyes.

"I—"

"He told me about how you broke her heart in such a vicious way. He told me about every single scar he discovered on her arms. He told me about how hurt she was: both mentally and emotionally. But the worst of it all? He told me about how much she actually loved you despiteb all of this. Even after all the cruel things you put her through, she loved you. She loved the boy hiding behind his demons."

"I'm sorry," I whispered, hiding my face behind my shaky hands as hot and salty tears began to roll down my cheeks. "I'm so sorry."

"Rose was a beautiful girl, Miles. I never had the chance to meet her in person, but even I can tell that she must have truly loved you. It's just very sad to know that she lost the battles against your demons. And it's even more sad to know that she kept fighting, even though she knew that she didn't have a chance to win at all. And now she's broken just like you." My father put his right hand on top of my knee and shot one of those 'I am sorry for you' looks at me which caused me to close my eyes in pain.

"I loved her too, dad. I swear I did. I just didn't realize it back then. I pulled her too deep into this mess I was stuck in and I had no damn idea about how much pain all of it would cause her until it was too late. I was too scared to admit that I used her for my own benefits. I was a coward. Instead of confronting her with the truth, I let her think that I was dating Josephine again. But—"

"But it hurt her even more than the actual truth probably would have." He finished the sentence for me while shaking his head in a disappointed way. "How could you do that, Miles? The worst feeling for a young girl is to feel unloved and you didn't even give her any other chance but to surrender. She put her weapons aside and let both of your demons consume her."

I wiped away the tears that were spilling down my face while my chin still trembled. "I hate myself so much. I honestly wish I could just diasppear. Just d—"

"Don't even dare to finish this sentence," he said, raising his voice. "Everything will work out fine for you, don't worry about it. You're young, son. You still have all of your life ahead of you. Josephine and Rose were just two dark chapters in your past but I promise you that all of this pain will be gone soon. All you need to do is tell Rose how sorry you are. Either tell her in person or try to reach out to her via... I don't know, social media maybe? Or be old-school and write a letter. I could hand it to her father or something. Does that sound alright for you?"

"I actually wrote about one hundred letters for her. I simply don't have the courage to reach out to her. I am anxious. I don't want to ruin her happiness or remind her of all the pain she had to endure because of me. She seems to be very happy right now and that's what gives me anxiety."

Rose somehow managed to get over her past and I was beyond proud of her achievement.

She was brave and strong but I already knew that. She always thought that she was a weak girl, but I was aware of all the strength she had in her bones. I could have never survived all the sick things that I put her through if I were her. She survived the darkness. She survived the hopelessnes. She survived the pain.

"There is nothing to be scared about. Just do it. I'm sure that she thinks about you sometimes. Women are wise. She probably already forgave you and is just waiting for you to apologize so that she can close this chapter once and for all." He squeezed my shoulder before he got up to walk towards my door.

"Dad?"

"Yeah?" he turned around one last time.

"Do you...do you think we could...we could be together again? As a couple I mean? Do you think she'd try it again with me?" My voice was shaking because I didn't really want to hear his answer to my question. But a little flicker of hope inside of me told me that my father would say something that would brighten up my day.

He looked down at the floor for a few seconds until his eyes met mine again. "No. I know this sounds harsh but I don't think that there is another chance for you two. You need to apologize and try to find yourself again. You need to work on yourself first. You need to heal in order to love again, Miles. It's up to Rose though. Maybe she's just waiting for a better version of the boy she used to love so much. Now go to sleep and rest. Everything will be fine."

And with those last words, he walked out of my room and closed the door behind him as he did so. I layed down on my bed and stared at the blank ceiling as some memories from my past kept rewinding in front of my eyes. I would never forget the day I saw Rose for the first time. I'll never forget the way her eyes sparkled and her heartbeat quickened whenever I was close to her. The way she pulled her lower lip between her front teeth whenever I touched her...

But sadly, I will also never forget the moment she spotted Josephine and I at our graduation. I will never forget the hurt in her eyes and the pain in her chest when she finally heard the truth from my lips. I will never forget how I broke her and that killed me inside.

I lost.

—

author's note:

Votes and comments have decreased immensly. And I know that it's mainly because I take years to update but it's still sad to see how I've lost some peeps who read this story. :(

A vote and a comment would make me the happiest.

Thank you from the bottom of my heart.

Chapter 12 - The Moment She Knew

- -

T ime will tell

I honestly couldn't believe that I was going to prom. This year had been the roughest year of my life and I just didn't feel like going to prom to be surrounded by people I didn't even care about in the first place. It had already been a few months since Rose and I "broke up" - only if you could call it that. I missed her a lot - a lot more than I actually thought I would when I started this game. She was different in a very good way and she liked, even loved, me although I was the biggest prick towards her.

It was crazy and I still didn't know what I did to deserve the love she gave me, but I was forced to ruin whatever we had. I couldn't bear to be close to her anymore because I didn't want to fall in love with her or catch any feelings towards her. I had a goal and I needed to accomplish that certain goal. It was for the best to split our ways and let her be herself again. I was already putting her through enough and I was not in the right state of mind to deal with her heartbreak once she found out that I only used her for my own benefits.

Rose was a good girl. She had a lot of love to give. She cared about everyone and always tried to help people but she had to love herself first. She was an easy catch and that's why it didn't take long for her to develop feelings for me. You just had to say a few nice things to her, take her to some beautiful places and basically just touch her and boom - she likes you.

I realized that I had to stop this game when I noticed her scars. She was in too deep and I had to pull her out but it was harder than I thought it would be. I didn't notice that I had fallen head over heels in love with this girl during the process of getting my payback. Everything felt different and better whenever I was close to her. She had this power, the ability to make me feel good but sadly, my demons still had the upper hand on me.

While she tried to save me from myself, she couldn't save herself from me. That was my wake-up call. I needed to distance myself from her. I had to let her go. I didn't deserve her and she didn't deserve any of this. I was destined to rot in hell after everything I put her through.

The secret phone calls, the secret messages - well, being secretive in general had to stop. Rose was smart. She was definitely feeling that something was wrong and that's why she kept doubting my words. Josephine tried to contact me. She was constantly messaging me about how much she missed me and all that stuff but I didn't buy any of her lies. I texted her just for fun. I wanted to fool her just to break her heart like she broke mine.

But then there was Rose. She was inbetween all of this mess, so I did what I should have done long ago: I broke up with her. Why? Because I reached what I wanted to reach: Make Andrew and Josephine jealous. Andrew was going nuts because there was nothing he could do. He was a coward. In order to warn Rose about me, he had to tell her about the fact that he cheated on her not once but twice but that's something he couldn't do.

I couldn't take my eyes off of Rose ever since she stepped foot into this auditorium. She looked exhausted but still so freaking beautiful and I truly just felt like embracing her in my arms until she'd fall asleep with her head pressed to my chest - like she used to.

"I wish I would have worn my hair down, don't you think?" Josephine asked after a few minutes of silence. I hated myself for doing this, but I just prayed for Rose not to see us although that was the plan all along. She'd move on from me quicklier if she saw Jo and I together again. And after this night, I'd tell Josephine to get out of my life once and for all. Even though Rose always told me to forgive and not to forget, I could neither forgive nor forget what she did to me. I simply dispised her. "Miles?"

I rolled my eyes before I focused on Rose again. "What?"

"Are you even listening to what I'm saying?" she sounded offended but I honestly didn't even care a slight bit.

I turned my head sideways to look her deep in the eyes as I said, "No."

"Okay why did you even invite me to accompany you to prom when you don't even want to be here with me?" she sounded offended and hurt. There was so much I wanted to tell her right now, but I pushed those thoughts aside.

"Is it that obvious?" I wondered.

She just nodded while grabbing a cheese cracker. "Pretty obvious. I thought you wanted to try again with me?"

I bit onto my bottom lip until it hurt. From the corner of my eyes I could see that Rose was walking towards the restroom and my heart nearly beat out of my chest as I watched her walk off like a goddess. I remained seated and tried to avoid whatever Josephine had to say next while listening to the songs they played.

After a while I noticed that it had been about twenty minutes since Rose left her group of "friends" to use the restroom but she hasn't returned yet, which made me feel a certain type of way because I couldn't spot Andrew on his seat either. Where did she go?

"Hold on, I need to pee." I cut Jo off and rushed towards the ladies restroom. I leaned my back against the wall next to the door and decided to wait for another five minutes until I'd ask some random girl to go check in on her.

I grew impatient but right before I had the chance to ask the girl who was about to walk into the restroom to wash her hands, the door swung open and the girl I was waiting for walked out. She didn't look good though. She seemed to be in deep thoughts as she massaged her temples and I had no idea what to do so I just stood in front of her with my paralyzed legs. Once she re-opened her blue eyes, they were met with mine and she looked just as confused as I probably did. I couldn't stop my eyes from trailing along her body until I reached her face because where she managed to hold me captive.

We continued to stare into and get lost in each others souls until I decided to break this akward silence between us. "You look different." was the first thing that popped into my mind and I wanted to slap myself for saying that as I tried to touch her shoulder but she jerked away immediately.

She swallowed the lump in her throat as she said, "You still look the same."

Her comment caused me to smile to myself but I noticed that she was still looking at me with those sparkling eyes. "You can't stop staring at me," I remarked to ease the tension but it didn't quite work the way I thought it would.

"And you can't stop staring at me," she contered fiercly. "What do you want from me anyway? Why did you talk to me?" Her voice was a mixture of pain, hurt, disappointment and anger - which I totally understood. She had every right to feel this way towards me.

I couldn't stop myself from smiling again. Although she was angry, she still looked super cute and I thought that was adorable. "Am I not allowed to talk to you anymore?"

"Miles," she sighed, shaking her head in sadness. "Too much has happened between us. It even hurts to look at you right now, so why did you appear in front of me? What do you want?" - and my smile dropped.

"I wanted to see you for the last time," I explained as I let out a loud breath I didn't even know I was holding. "This is our final goodbye."

She played with her thumbs and pulled her eyebrows together. "Then this is the only chance to ask you about this."

"Ask me about what?" I wondered with confusion written all over my face. I turned around to make sure that Jo wasn't looking after me or she'd ruin this moment.

"Ask you about your fight with Andrew last year," she said. "Miles I want you to be honest to me at least for once in your life."

My whole body felt tense now. "There is nothing to be honest about." I shrugged nonchalantly but I could already feel the sweat forming on my forehead as I licked my lips nervously. "We fought and thats it."

She scoffed, "Oh really? Why did you fight though? Can you please be more precise?"

My eyes roamed around the room behind her because her eyes were the last place I wanted to look at right now. And suddenly, I spotted the person who started all of this. "Ask him yourself," I pointed behind her.

"Rose," Andrew shouted from a few feet away, rushing towards us. "We've been waiting outside for you." He seemed to be mad at her which made me ball my right hand into a fist. But once he noticed my presence, his annoyance towards Rose vanished and was replaced by anger towards me. "And what are you doing here? Don't you think you already hurt her enough?"

I looked at him and shook my head slowly. "You're pathetic, Andrew."

Rose jumped between us and when she grabbed his hand, I sucked my bottom lip between my teeth to calm down. "Why did you fight him at a party last summer? He couldn't be honest to me," she said pointing at me. "Can you?"

I scoffed, "Do you honestly expect him to be honest to you? He has been lying to you ever since—" I knew that if I finished this sentence, I would hurt her, so I shut up immediately.

Without further hesitation, Andrew grabbed me by the collar of my shirt and pressed me against the wall behind us. "Don't you even dare! "

"Hey!" Rose shouted while trying to pull Andrew away from me. "I deserve to hear the truth, so tell me damnit!" She seemed to be exhausted and I honestly just felt like wrapping my arms around her but I had to get this through.

Andrew and I stared into each other's eyes and I couldn't even put into words how much I despised him. Although it was going to be extremely painful for her, I had to tell her the damn truth. I had to stop being a coward and tell her why we were in this position right now. I nodded as my heartbeat increased. "I'll be honest. It all started because of him," I whispered helplessly. "Please believe me when I tell you that I did not want things to go like this."

Rose closed her eyes for a brief moment. "What does that mean?"

My entire body was shaking, so I scratched my neck deeply to stop it somehow before I covered my face with both of my hands. How was I supposed to tell her any of this? How was I supposed to break her? I had to make sure that she believed me, even if it meant to tell her the biggest lie I ever had to tell anyone. I gathered my strength together as I said, "I never had feelings for you."

Right as those crucial words left my lips, she gasped. Her chest was rising up and down oh so rapidly that I thought she would pass out any minute from now. I could see how she was breaking inside and that made me want to scream. Even tears were rolling down her rosy cheeks now and she turned her face away from me. "You never had feelings for me?" she asked barely above a whisper.

I inhaled, "I'm sorry, but—"

"No, I don't need your empathy!" she cried with all her voice while holding her hand up to silence me. "Why?"

I suddenly couldn't do this. I decided to remain silent until Andrew would decide to jump in and talk for me. I was hoping that he was making up excuses in his head so that we could all shake hands and walk back home to forget this moment ever happened.

"Can you explain this? Did you know about any of this?" Andrew was in deep thought as he looked at her with sad eyes while she hit his chest aggressively.

I pinched myself to continue. "You were at the wrong place during the right time. I mean I really enjoyed your company sometimes, but I- I just never had any romantic feeling for you. I'm sorry."

This situation was getting the best of me. I simply wanted to punch myself unconscious and escape this torture. She put her small hand right on top of her heart and looked at Andrew who still remained silent. "Andrew?"

"I was heartbroken, Rose. I was absolutely heartbroken. I mean I'm thankful that you've been there for me but it's not in our hands who we choose to fall in love with." I tried to explain again and this time, she kinda got it.

Her eyes grew twice their size when she realized what I had done. "Oh my god, did you use me? Talk to me!"

Now I was extremely nervous. Our eyes connected for a split second before I turned sideways to look at Andrew because I really needed his help now. "He never stopped loving Jo," were the only words he mumbled while staring at the floor beneath us. "He has always been in love with her."

"What is going on here?" I heard a familiar voice shout from behind and once I realized who this voice belonged to, I wanted to just knock myself out for real. But maybe it was better this way. Maybe it was easier for Rose to erase me from her life once and for all. Maybe it was easier for her to move on. So I did what I never thought I'd do ever again. "Babe!"

"Babe?" Rose repeated with the most heartbroken voice I had ever heard as she looked me deep in the eyes.

"Look—"

"I—" her voice broke completely. She was covering her mouth with both of her hands while closing her eyes. "I was a rebound for you, wasn't I? While you were waiting for her to return back to you or to want you back, you needed someone you could play with, someone who could entertain you and give you what you needed until she would eventually come back to you."

"You've got it right, Rose." Andrew chimed in, which caused Rose to take a step back to increase the space between the three of us. She didn't look good and I couldn't even endure to think about what she might be going through right now. What I was doing was merciless and I knew that I'd end up in hell because of this. This was crucial.

"I didn't know that I would hurt you so much," I whispered. "I'm just sorry Rose. I'm so sorry about this." And I truly was. I meant what I said from the bottom of my heart. I was sorry. An apology couldn't fix any of this, but I still wanted her to know that I was deeply sorry for everything I had put her through.

"Guys what's going on?" Jo asked, moving closer to us. I intertwined our hands and felt beyond disgusted by myself as I did so.

"I'll tell you when we get back home. Don't worry about any of this, okay?" I told her although I knew damn well that I would not take her home with me.

Rose sobbed, "Why did you choose me as your victim? What did I ever do to you that you thought I deserve this?" It hurt to look at her. I was done. I couldn't endure this pain.

"Now it's your turn to talk, Andrew." I nudged his ribs with my elbow. "Tell her."

"Oh my god," she sobbed uncontrollably. "You knew this, didn't you? You freaking knew about all of this!" I could see that she was slowly counting one plus one together in her head. "You knew about all of this and still pretended to care about me and I believed you."

"Revenge." Andrew spat with disgust lacing on his voice. "For him it was all about revenge because he thought I was dating his girlfriend behind his back even though I was not."

I rolled my eyes, "Oh shut up dude. You have always been unfaithful, don't even try to tell me otherwise."

He let out an exasperated sigh. "Why can't you just believe me? I didn't date Jo, okay? I did not date her, I didn't! Get that into your sick mind already!" This time, he averted his gaze towards the girl next to me while shaking his head. "You still couldn't tell him Josephine?" Instead of responding to his question, she tried to hide behind me.

"You honestly expect me to believe someone who cheated on his girlfriend twice? I caught you red-handed, dude." I cut in.

We were so focused on tearing each other down, that we forgot about Rose's presence completely until she chimed in with a weakened voice, "What?"

"He cheated on you too!" I yelled, pointing straight towards him to feel better about myself. "He slept with your best friend. Once a cheater, always a cheater."

Andrew was shocked because he obviously didn't expect me to drop the news like this, which was quite amusing. "Rose, I swear—"

"What?!" she shouted louder. "Andrew?" Within the blink of an eye, she pushed him with every ounce of strength left in her - she pushed him so hard that he nearly tripped and fell down onto the cold hard ground. The two of us were caught off-guard at her sudden outburst and had no idea what we were supposed to do now. And just a second later she was standing right in front of me. I could feel her hot breath on my face as she stared at me with her heartbroken eyes. "You put me through all of this because of her?"

I tried to calm her by placing my hands on top of her shoulders, but she just shoved me against the wall behind us, which caused Jo to flinch. "Don't touch me!" she screamed louder than ever before. "Don't ever touch me again!"

"He wanted to make me jealous of you by making you fall out of love with me and fall in love with him instead." Andrew took a cautious step forward this time after he managed to re-adjust himself. "Jo was unhappy and I was her friend. At least I tried to be her friend during times Miles was being the ignorant prick he is. He told Jo he loved her all the time - which I believed, but he hurt her so much. These two were toxic for each other and their relationship was unhealthy."

"Miles is that true?" Josephine wondered. "You had something going on with this girl? You used her to hurt us?" she motioned between Andrew and herself with disbelief written all over her face.

"I didn't realize that during the process of supporting Jo, she fell in love with me. I admit that we kissed a few times when she called me in the middle of the night to cry her eyes out on my shoulder, but I didn't return her feelings because I have always just been in love with one girl in my entire life. And this girl is you, Rose."

"Oh shut—" I honestly couldn't listen to his nonsense any longer. He clearly admitted that he cheated on her and he also couldn't deny the previous accusations, so I couldn't understand why he was still trying to fix things with her oh so hopelessly.

"I—"

This time, she held both of her shaking hands up to silence the two of us. "You two," she sniffed, licking her lips wet. "You two disgust me. I can't believe you two involved me in this sick twisted game of yours. I can't believe that the two of you used me like this, broke and hurt me like this. You put me through all this pain, made me hate myself, made me hate life like this... I just can't believe you did this. I have no idea what I did to deserve this, what I did to experience this, what I did to become your target but I know for a fact that I loved both of you during different times of my life. Can you believe this? I actually loved you."

"But Rose—"

Instead of hearing him out, she shouted, "Stop! It was all about revenge from the very beginning. You planned this, didn't you?" she spoke directly towards me. "I finally understand now. You captured my attention, stole my journal and then even somehow managed to get yourself into my house to make it even easier for you to make me fall in love with you step by step, right? That's also why you always asked me about Andrew and didn't want me to hang around him, am I right?"

Yes, you are absolutely right, Rose. She started to clap both of her hands together slowly. "Congratulations. I congratulate you for pretending to care about me although you never did." She looked at Andrew while speaking those words. "And I applaud you for breaking my heart in the cruelest way possible, Miles Reese. No matter where I go, what I do or how old I get, I will always remember you, your name and the pain you put me through because I have these deep scars on my body, mind and heart that will always remind me of you." Her words cut deeper than knives and it was hard for me to be standing opposite her any longer.

And that's why I escaped.

—

author's note:

Necessary chapter, folks. I guess the next chapter could be quite interesting, so keep an eye out on that since I'm trying to update this story faster!

Oh and I'm working on a new story, so make sure to check it out once it's published (it's called 'Dancing With A Stranger')!

A vote and a comment are appreciated.

Much love.

Chapter 13 - A Foolish Game

T ime will tell

"There you are," A female voice called out from behind me as she moved closer towards my direction. Her heels were clicking against the concrete floor beneath us and I could hear her let out a groan once she approached me.

"Here I am," I sighed out loud while removing myself from my current position to turn around to face her.

"What was that all about, Miles?" Although it was mid-August, the nights were already freezing cold and now that she wasn't wearing a jacket, she was shivering like crazy.

"Honestly Josephine? Just get lost. I'm sick of you. Sick of this. Sick of everything." I was still trying to calm myself down after everything that just happened inside this stupid auditorium. The truth was finally revealed, but under what prize? Even though I had won this foolish game of mine, I somehow still managed to be the loser of the night. Instead of actually winning anything, I had lost everything.

She looked at me with a blank facial expression as she crossed her arms in front of her chest. "Wait- me too? You didn't mean anything you said last night?"

I rolled my eyes at her stupidity while taking a step forward to look her straight into the eyes that once meant the world to me, but now I was just staring into some blue orbs with no meaning at all. "Could you really be that stupid? Of course I did not. You cheated on me with my former best friend. And even though you're here with me right now, your heart is still beating for him. I may be a fool, but not for you."

"Miles—"

"Spare me your lies. You're the worst thing that ever happened to me, Josephine. I despise you more than I despise myself and I don't even know whether that's possible. Even looking at you makes me vomit right here, right now. Disappear. Go!" Since the game was over, I didn't have to pretend to care about her any longer. I was surprised that she actually thought that I would give her a second chance after everything she put me through.

"You ididot!" I heard someone shout from behind me for the second time tonight, and as I was about to turn around to face that certain person, his fist connected with my jaw straight away. "Are you happy now? Did you reach your pathetic goal? Did you get what you want? Tell me!" I had to take a minute to process that he just hit me. Andrew was a pacifist, he was against violence but still decided to hit me which only proved to me that he was deeply hurt and truly angry.

He was spitting fire. His chest was rising up and down in such a fast pace that I actually thought he was going to explode. This was the first time in almost four years that I had seen him like this. He was usually known for his calm persona, but apparently he had a darker side as well. I rubbed my jaw gently and noticed some blood on my fist as I did so. Although I myself was mad, angry - furious even - I didn't have the strength in me to fight anyone tonight. I was done with everything and that's why I decided not to hit back but remain on my spot on the ground instead.

"Rose was already facing so many tough obstacles in her life because of you and now you truly managed to break her! Why did you have to tell her all of this? Especially on a night like this? Do you even care about the fact that you ruined her teenage years?" Andrew continued to shout at me but I knew him all too well. His voice broke after he finished his last sentence and he let his body fall down onto the park bench next to us while covering his face with both of his shaky hands.

"Andrew, please calm down." Josephine rushed next to him but he jerked away immediately after she tried to touch his face. She was such a pathetic piece of humanity that I couldn't help but let out a loud scoff.

Andrew licked his lips and closed his eyes briefly before he held his hand out in front of her face, "You need to stop this nonsense once and for all. Don't get me wrong but I'm so tired of dealing with you."

"So am I," I whispered in front of me before my head connected with the cold pavement. I was tired and extremely exhausted. This night got the best of me and I just wanted to close my eyes and disappear forever. I looked up at the stars but they weren't shining as bright as they used to and I had a feeling that it would start to rain any minute from now.

"What's wrong with you two?" Josephine went off. "Why are you both trying to put the blame on me? I don't even know that girl yet here you are blaming me for everything that just happened!"

"Well, that's because you freaking caused this mess!" Andrew yelled at her. "You were the one who caused this maniac to ruin our lives, so thank you from the bottom of my heart for that," he said pointing at me. "You were the coward who couldn't tell him about your sick obsession with me. You were the coward who lied to him about us. You couldn't tell him that you literally forced me to kiss you that night at the party where he caught us - and instead of admitting the truth to him, you chose to lie and blame it on me!" The sound of his fist connecting with the trash can right next to him caused me to jump back up.

I rubbed my eyes to have a clear vision and glanced at the two of them in a new light. Why did I even let them control my life for the past year? Why didn't I just hold my middle finger up high and tell both of them to get lost and carried on with my life like I should have? Why did I give them all the power to ruin me like this? "In all honesty, what happened that night at the party? Is this true Josephine? Is he innocent?"

"Tell him Josephine, I'm begging you. You're not aware of the damage you caused, are you?" Andrew pleaded and I narrowed my eyes at her while listening to his words.

She swallowed hard. "Okay, okay. It's true, damnit! Andrew is innocent. It's...I did all of this. You're right, apparently all of this is my fault."

"Be more precise." I could feel some anger boil inside of but I really didn't want it to take control of me tonight or ever again, so I exhaled out loud and tried to prepare myself for what she was about to confess.

"I was jealous of Andrew and his relationship to that girl Rose...I think that's what her name was, right? I was jealous because he treated her like a princess. He loved her so deeply. He cared about her from the bottom of his heart. She meant everything to him. I was jealous of that. I'm in no way saying that you didn't love me Miles, because I know you did. But we didn't have the fairytale kind of love. We argued too much. We hurt each other too often. Screamed at each other too many times. It was exhausting. I kept up with all of this because I loved you or I thought I did, I still don't know. But let me tell you one thing," she said holding her index finger up high while trying to hold back her tears. "There is a difference between being in love with someone and forcing yourself to think that you love someone."

I pushed my eyebrows together and shook my head slowly to comprehend what she just said. "Keep talking."

"I was used to you and therefore, I was scared to be on my own again once you leave me. I didn't want to lose you, Miles, but I also didn't want to be in this toxic relationship with you any longer. I simply couldn't deal with you anymore and needed to escape from you."

"And you escaped to Andrew," I finished her sentence. The more I thought about her words, the more they made sense to me.

She nodded, wiping her tears from under her eyes as she continued. "Although Andrew was just trying to be a friend to me, I couldn't stop myself from developing feelings towards him. You have no idea how hard it was to be close to him but not being able to touch him or feel him and when we kissed for the very first time, electricity raced through my entire body and soul. He managed to ignite a fire in me. I felt alive again - he made me feel alive again. And that's when I realized that I, in fact, didn't love you anymore." She was constantly digging her nails deep into her palms and I could tell that she was scared about admitting all of this since she knew too damn well that I had anger issues, but as for tonight, I just wanted to listen to her explain all of this.

I nodded for her to continue.

"He was in a relationship around that time and I knew that he loved her with his whole entire heart. He talked about her so often and whenever he did, sparks were flying in his eyes and around the room and his heart was racing like crazy. He was genuinely happy, Miles. And that was the worst part of it: the jealousy. I wanted to be the girl he loved. I wanted to be the girl he talked about on a daily basis. I wanted to be the girl he wrote poems about. I wanted to be her."

"And when you realized that you'd never replace her, you lied to me?" I chimed in because I had heard enough. "When you realized that you couldn't have him, you came back to me. And when I caught you two that night, you put all the blame on him so that I-" I cut myself off to drive a hand through my hair because I could count one plus one together now.

"You should have just let me explain everything to you that night instead of busting my face open, Miles. You should have known that I would have never done anything as crucial as this to you but you simply decided to solve this with violence like you always did." Andrew had a point - a pretty good one at that. I should have listened to him. I should have let him explain. I should have tried to solve this verbally and not with violence. "I meant what I said inside. There is only one girl I have ever truly loved in my entire life and that girl is Rose."

"I can't believe this." Was all I managed to say because I was at a loss for words. To put it all short: I became the victim of a lie.

"You better believe it though. And because of all of this, you hurt an innocent soul instead. You hurt a girl who had nothing to do with any of this. You hurt a girl who actually cared about you and that's your real loss tonight, Miles. You lost a diamond you never even deserved in the first place and now try to deal with that," he said as he was about to leave but turned around one last time. "It's hard to admit this, but she freaking loved you. And I truly wonder what you two would have become if you were a better man." And with those last words, he left.

Josephine and I remained right at our spots for another few minutes until she whispered, "I apologize for all of this. I'm...I'm so sorry. I hope someday you can find a girl who will love you with her whole heart again because you deserve all the love you can get." Right after those words escaped from her lips, she decided to leave as well. "Goodbye Miles, farewell."

Now I was left on my own again - like I was used to. And as I predicted earlier, I could hear the sound of a thunder and not even a couple of seconds later, rain came pouring down causing me to drown in my own misery.

—

author's note:

EXCUSE ANY TYPOS OR SENTENCES THAT DON'T MAKE ANY SENSE.

I wrote this chapter within three hours, I'm proud of myself. The next chapter is going to be in present tense again, so yeah prepare yourself for what's about to come.

PS a vote and a comment would make me the happiest girl (especially since it's my birthday tomorrow!), so do your job hah!

I'm sending much love.

Chapter 14 - Home

Time will tell

    I woke up quite early today since I spent the whole night tossing and turning in my bed. My thoughts were keeping me up all night and I couldn't stop thinking about what my father told me. He was right and I knew it. I had to apologize - it was the least I could do and as much as I tried to run away from my duties, I was forced to man up now. And since I never liked social media, I decided to write a letter instead.

Even though I already tried to write the perfect letter to her a hundred times, I never managed to express my feelings the way I wanted to and that made me angry. My anxiety was literally eating me alive and I was sick of feeling this way. I wanted to- no, I had to- heal. I had to get this over with. I had to take full responsibility for all the cruel things I did. I had to take full responsibility for my actions. I was a grown man now and it was time for me to act this way too.

I leaned back against my chair and grabbed my phone from my nightstand. My thumb was shaking as I pressed the instagram button again after weeks of being absent and searched for Rose's profile. I noticed that she uploaded a new picture and my heart nearly dropped out of my chest as I hesitated to tap on it. Once I managed to overcome my fear, I was blown away by her beauty again. She kept getting more beautiful each time I saw a picture of her and I wondered how that was possible. How was she even real?

As I stared at the picture, I somehow started to think about the year I met her. I started to think about the year I changed, about the year I became a completely different person. I started to think about all the people I had hurt throughout my life. I couldn't change the past, or perhaps my past, but I could change the future. I could change how people viewed and judged me. I could try to change their perspective and make them see me in a new light.

I rushed towards my wardrobe and grabbed one of my many black hoodies and a pair of washed jeans before I got dressed. A quiet knock on my door made me turn around only to be met with my father once again. "Good morning."

"Good morning, dad." I greeted while buttoning my jeans. "How did you know that I wasn't sleeping?" It must be around eight o'clock and I had been up for about three hours now and simply wondered how he knew that I was up. I usually slept till noon and left the house until after midnight.

"I could hear you," he said as he stepped inside. "How did you sleep?"

Once I was ready, I sat down onto the edge of my bed and sighed. "Not so well. I think I slept for an hour or maybe two before my thoughts got the best of me."

"Have you been feeling like this ever since you left for college?" he asked, taking a seat right next to me. "We're going to fix this, you know that right? You'll be able to sleep peacefully again, Miles. I promise."

A small smile curved my lips for a few seconds before it turned into a frown. "I hope so, dad. Life is tough and sometimes, it can get the best of you.

And it has a very cruel way of torturing you with your own mind. I wish there was a switch I could turn off once and for all but that would be too easy." I was exhausted. This constant monologue in my head was driving me insane and I just wanted to silence the voice inside of me but there was no instruction how to.

"You know, when I was younger I met a girl. She was pretty and I spent the whole day just thinking about her. I spent the whole day thinking about how my life would be if she was in it. I spent my whole day thinking about what she might like, what her favorite color might be, or her favorite book and so on. And when I tried to sleep, my mind didn't let me. I couldn't turn my thoughts off, so I stayed up all night thinking about how I could capture her attention." A huge smile was spread across his face as he kept talking and I listened carefully.

"Did it work?" I wondered, scratching my neck.

He raised his left hand and pointed at the ring on his ring-finger. "I married her."

"Mom?!" I asked in bewilderment.

He nodded, "Yes. Sometimes, our thoughts help us gain the courage we think we don't have. This is complex and so weird to explain or even understand but I just want you to know that you are couragous. You are smart and you are strong, Miles. Your thoughts may be driving you insane right now, but they are just trying to show you a direction. And your certain direction is Rose. Make peace with her and you will make peace with your past - maybe not to 100%, but enough peace to be able to move on."

"That's what I'm about to do. I'm going outside. I want to walk through the neighborhood and...apologize to everyone I ever hurt. A small step into the right direction, right?" I had no idea how many people I ever hurt or where they might be today, but I still wanted to make sure that I said those words and got rid of this burden on my back.

"I'm proud of you. You've grown up so much and it shows. Be back home before dinner, alright? I've talked with your mother and she might have a few things to say to you as well."

I smiled, "Thanks dad. Your support means the most to me."

...

Walking through the once familiar streets in my home town brought back a ton of memories. I used to run around this neighbourhood from dusk til dawn when I was younger. We used to spent our time running around here with my friends, trying to catch each other as seven year olds. We used to buy ice cream from an ice cream truck in summer and strolled around town with our skateboards and bicycles while laughing out loud.

We used to have snow fights in winter and waterbomb fights in summer. We used to drink hot chocolate in autumn and self-made smoothies in spring. We were friends, brothers, family even. We were unseperable. We couldn't go without each other and that's why we spent every single minute of every day together. We were friendship goals until we reached a crossroads. Every single one of us chose a different direction and our paths never crossed again ever since then.

"Miles?" I looked up immediately when I heard someone say my name. "Is that you?"

I was met with two hazel eyes and it took me a few seconds to figure out who the person in front of me was. "Mr. Peterson?" The last time I saw this man was probably six years ago and I was amazed by the fact that he still managed to look so young.

"I didn't know that you were back in town. Are you visiting your parents during winter break?" he asked, taking off his gloves. "Mike came down here for a week and left again. I bet he would have stayed a bit longer if he knew that you'd come back home as well."

I forced a smile on my face and just nodded my head. Mike and I hadn't spoken in over eight years - if you don't count the greetings - because we simply grew apart. "Uhm yeah," I said while scratching my head. "How has he been? Is everything alright?"

"He's doing amazing. He has a couple more months to go until he finally graduates and I honestly can't wait. He's very happy in New York and already found a place he can work at once he's done going to University. What about you?" He guided me over to the porch where we both sat down and I wondered whether Mike still had the necklace we all bought at a vintage store in late August when we were nine.

"That's fantastic, fingers crossed everything works out fine for him. Hearing this really makes me happy, but I kinda always knew that he would make if far in life," I admitted truthfully. Even though we didn't manage to keep in touch over these years, I was beyond proud of him and his achievements in life. "I have one more year to go until I hopefully graduate."

He smiled wholeheartedly while patting my back. "I saw your father a couple of weeks ago when Mike was here and he kept asking about you. I'm glad that you're doing fine, Miles. After all, you used to be like the ninth child I never had," he chuckled and I joined him once I got the reference he made.

"Can you do me a favor?" I asked once we stopped laughing.

"Of course," he said, turning around to face me.

"Can you tell Mike that I'm sorry?"

His smile turned into a confused facial expression. "Sorry for what exactly?"

I had no idea what I was apologizing for, but I could remember that we used to fight sometimes when we were kids and I just wanted to make sure that he knew that I was sorry for all the times that I may have hurt him. "Just tell him that I am."

After a few seconds of silence he rubbed his beard. "I will."

"Thank you. I should get going now but it was great to catch up with you again, Mr. Peterson. Stay well!"

...

On my way home, I stumbled upon a person I truly wasn't prepared for and I honestly had no idea how to react. We both stopped in our tracks and just stared at each other with wide eyes and confusion written all over our faces. She blinked a few times to make sure that she wasn't actually seeing a ghost, but in fact me standing right opposite her small figure. "Miles...you—you are back?"

I groaned as I put my hands in the pockets of my jeans. "I'll be leaving in a couple of days."

"I—" she seemed to be at a loss for words and I didn't blame her because I was feeling the exact same way. My mind went blank when she appeared in front of me simply because she was the last person I thought I would ever see again. I didn't even know how to feel right now, because usually I felt hatred towards her, but now? Now I couldn't spot any hatred but peace instead. "You...uhm...how—how are you?" I could see how nervous she was by the way she kept folding her arms in front of her chest only to unfold them again to play with her thumbs instead.

I didn't listen to her or focus on whatever she was saying because I was busy making my mind up. I was searching for the right words to say but I couldn't form a single coherent sentence in my head let alone speak one out. And then my gaze landed on the diamond ring on her left hand as she kept moving her arms, which caused me to push my eyebrows together in utter bewilderment and ignore her question completely. "What's that?" I asked astonished while pointing at her finger.

She was caught off-guard when she noticed what I was looking at. "Oh- that?" her lips were quivering and her cheeks turned a dark shade of red as she scratched her arm. "I...I got engaged in September last year."

Once those words escaped from her lips and digged their way through my brain, I realized that time was flying by quite fast. I couldn't believe that I dated this girl five years ago and planned a future with her —a future that turned into the past. I couldn't hold back a chuckle when I thought about how freaking weird life was. One day you think you will marry someone and have kids with them and the next day you despise this person with your whole being. One day life is great and the next day everything you built comes tumbling down right in front of you. One day you're happy, the next day you're not.

And then realization hit me again. It had been three long years since all of it happened. Three years. I had to let that sink in. Everything had changed ever since then. We grew up. We changed. We became wiser. "Congra— congratulations, Josephine. I... I'm genuinely happy for you." I was surprised at my reaction but somehow, that was exactly what I wanted to say because I was happy for her. I guess after all the messed up things we put each other through, at least one of us deserved to find the peace and serenity we were looking for so desperately. "You deserve it."

She obviously wasn't expecting to hear this from me since her mouth formed an 'o' and once our eyes connected, I could spot a thousand different emotions in them but I had struggles to figure out even one. "Thank you, Miles. I...uhm...I—" and then she couldn't hold her tears in any longer. "I'm so sorry."

Within seconds, she turned away from me and put both of her hands in front of her face before she began to cry out very loud. I was overwhelmed by this situation and hesitated because I was too confused by all of this. "Hey, Jo," I tried to calm her as I took a step forward to reach out for her. "Jo, look at me." Her hysterical cries were echoing through the neighbour-hood until I grabbed her arm gently to make her face me again. "Stop crying," I said slowly while cupping her warm cheeks with my cold hands.

She continued to sob while wiping her tears away with the back of her right hand. "It's just...I- I don't manage to be happy, Miles. I feel like I'm cursed. My fianceé gives me a thousand reasons to be happy about, but everytime I try to let his happiness consume me, I keep thinking about you and my mood drops instantly."

"Because of what happened?" I wondered although I already knew the answer to my question. I was kind of feeling bad for her. I mean yes, she played a huge part in all the chaos from the past, but she was younger then. I've been going - and am still going - through whatever she went through and I know that after a while, you won't be able to carry the huge burden on your back anymore —especially not on your own.

"Yes. I hate myself for everything I put you and everyone else through and that's why I can't be happy anymore. If I could go back in time...I would. Believe me, I would. I wouldn't even hesitate a single second and go back to change everything immediately. I would change the day you and I met. I would change the day you fell in love with me. I would change it all...but I can't. I swear if I had any power or some say in any of this, I would make you fall in love with her instead of me and—"

"Josephine," I drove both of my hands through my hair and closed my eyes while doing so. "Let go of the past. I understand how you're feeling right now because I feel the exact same b—"

She cut me off as she started to cry for the second time within ten minutes, "but you feel this way because of me. I'm the head of this mess, don't you get it? If it wouldn't have been for me, none of this would have happened."

"You need to make peace with the past and learn to let go. I know that I blamed you for most of this mess, but there is no other person I should blame other than me. Yes, you have hurt me. Yes, you have broken me and yes, you've turned my life upside down, but," I emphasized. "I chose to do all those cruel things to her, that didn't have anything to do with you."

"Don't even dare to put the blame on yourself again!" she screamed which caused me to remain silent. "I can only manage to be happy if I know that you're doing good, Miles."

I smiled slightly, staring up at the blue sky above us. "I'm on my way to recovery, Jo."

—

author's note:

I don't even know why I decided to cut the chapter off right there, but I thought that the situation seemed to be perfect? Idk. Well, we're one step closer to Miles reaching out to Rose!!! I can't even explain how nervous that makes me omg.

A vote and a comment are much, much appreciated you lovely people.

Much love from me to you :)

Chapter 15 - An Unexpected Arrival

T ime will tell

Sadly, it was time for me to fly back to Pennsylvania since my winter break was over and classes were about to start again. I had the most wonderful time with my family and was extremely happy that I finally managed to apologize for all the wrong that I had done to them. But I was even happier about the fact that I managed to build a good relationship to my mother and to have an even stronger bond with my father now. Those two meant the whole entire world to me and I was relieved to have them back in my life because I realized that I needed them the most.

Once I payed the taxi driver and ran all across the campus to reach my dorm, I was met with a very anxious Baldwin walking from the window to the wall in a fast pace. I guess he didn't even notice my presence in the room, so I pulled my eyebrows together in confusion. "Did you not miss me?" I asked, dropping my bags to the floor while opening my arms for him to hug me. I felt better — way better than I did when I left to visit my family, way better than two weeks ago and I was damn proud of myself.

He looked at me in horror while fiddling with his thumbs. It took him a couple of seconds before he walked over to hug me and I wondered why he was behaving like this. "Uh- uh hello Miles. I- uhm I'll use the restroom."

I let him walk past me while turning around to follow his fragile body disappear in the bathroom. After five minutes, I knocked on the door. "Are you alright, mate?"

He didn't respond for another minute. "I did something bad."

I wasn't sure whether I just heard him correctly, so I put my ear closer to the door that separated us in order to listen to him carefully. "What?" I asked, narrowing my eyes at the pot that was placed right next to me.

"I said I did something bad. You'll hate me for it," he said and I could literally hear the fear in his voice, which made me nauseous. Baldwin was a smart guy, I honestly couldn't understand any of his words. "I...I'm sorry Miles."

"Baldwin," I sighed, balling my fists in order to stay calm and not panic because I was damn scared. "Can you please open the door and talk to me face-to-face? I'm begging you. Nothing you say makes any sense to me right now."

"I can't!" He shouted in fear. "You'll kill me, I know you will."

I placed both of my hands onto the grey-silverish metal door and let out a loud breath. "I won't hurt you. Open the door and come out of there. Please Baldwin, don't be afraid." Somehow, my throat felt very dry and I had a nasty feeling in my stomach. I had an idea about what he might have done, but as for now I just prayed to dear God that he did not do what I currently think he did.

"Promise you won't hurt me, Miles? I am really scared." I could barely hear the last part because he was whispering, which caused me to close my eyes to continue to stay calm. Whatever he did, I wouldn't even dare to harm him in any way and I felt kind of offended that he thought that I'd hurt him.

"I promise," I finally said while letting out another breath I didn't know I was holding. My heart was beating so fast that I had problems to breathe properly. It kept hitting my rib cage until it eventually began to hurt.

The sound of the key turning inside the lock caused me to focus on Baldwin again. He hesitated a bit before he opened the door slowly. "Don't punch me, don't punch me, don't—"

He was shielding his eyes with his arms as he stood there with a quivering body, which caused me to shake my head at him. "I told you that I won't hurt you, stop it."

"Miles, I did some—"

"Something bad, I know. You've told me already. Be more precise, what did you do, Baldwin? I am curious to know and if you don't tell me right now, I will freak out. What did you do?" I repeated. My hands were shaking and I couldn't make it stop. I couldn't even describe this feeling of anxiety right now because a million different thoughts were racing through my mind and I was about to lose it.

"I did some sort of research on Rose and her boyfriend. I...I messaged him and asked whether he'd like to meet me— uhm you, I mean of course and he agreed. He is on his way to Pennsylvania Miles and he'll be here very soon." When those words left his mouth, I couldn't believe my own two ears. I couldn't believe what I had just heard. I couldn't believe what he just told me. I simply couldn't believe it.

My lips formed a weird smile and I really felt like laughing out loud. "Are you— are you kidding me right now, Baldwin? Is this some sort of joke? Are you freaking insane?"

He swallowed very hard while shaking his head. "I did it for you. Please don't be mad! That idea popped up in my mind when you were gone and I just wanted to help you. I know how much she means to you, but she has a boyfriend and maybe you could...I don't know...work things out with him first before you contact—"

"Baldwin!" I shouted, covering my face with both of my shaky hands. This had to be another nightmare. Rose's boyfriend was on his way to meet me? Why? Why would he want to meet me? Did Rose tell him about me? If she did, what did she told him about me and about us? How much did he know? "I can't believe you. I trusted you with this sensitive topic. You knew how hard it was for me to open up about it— hell, it took me three freaking years to tell you about her and you...you ruined it."

Although I loved Baldwin like a brother, I was absolutely mad and extremely disappointed in him. I mean yes, he tried to help me but he could've talked to me before doing something stupid like this. I was the fool in this story and I was not prepared to meet the guy who was in a relationship with the girl I deeply loved. "Miles, I'm so sorry. I only want the best for you and I'm still positive that meeting him will help you immensely, but if you don't, I can call him in your name again and—"

"In my name again? Did you message him in my name? Does he actually think that I messaged him? What if he told Rose about this!? Baldwin, what did you do!? How am I suppossed to get out of this mess now?! I—" I was outraged. This situation kept getting worse each passing second and per usual, I felt like disappearing once and for all. This was embarrassing and quite humiliating.

He nodded, placing his palms on his red cheeks. I could read the guilt that was written on his face each time I looked at him. "Miles, please meet him. If you don't feel better afterwards, you can punch me on the nose and I won't even be mad."

I kept shaking my head in disbelief. "I am disappointed in you and I want you to know that. I thought we were friends. I thought you sympathized with me. I thought you wanted to help me. You can't just walk around and try to fix broken hearts like this, okay?"

"But I do want to help you!"

I let out a frustrated growl as I sat down onto my bed while burying my face in my hands during the process. "Great job." I obviously didn't want to meet her obnoxious boyfriend and I truly couldn't seem to understand why he wanted to meet me so desperately.

"I—" Baldwin was cut off by the sound of his phone receiving an alert, which also caused me to take a short glimpse at him through my fingers.

He looked at me in utter shock and fear. "What?" I asked, panic lacing on my voice as well.

"He's here."

—

author's note:

BOOM. Okay, first things first: I'm begging you guys not to comment 'please update'. I'm doing my best to update as fast as I possibly can and sometimes, it takes longer. I personally don't like the outcomes of my previous chapters simply because I've been stuck with writers block for the past months and I keep losing readers because of it.

I always get spammed with 'when are you going to update?' or 'Update!' every time I post a new chapter and I think that's sort of disrespectful because those people who do that (not all but some!!!) are the same people who don't even vote in the first place. I write this story for you guys and I put a lot of effort into each chapter (although it doesn't show, I know), but whether you believe it or not, a simple vote or a simple comment have the ability to make me unbelievably happy.

The readers and the votes (and the comments) have gone downhill and that makes me extremely sad and anxious. I'm not as motivated as I used to be and I'm sorry for that, but I will continue for all those of you who decided to stay. I owe it all to you, so thank you from the deepest part of my heart for still being here.

Much love from me to you.

PS does anyone remember what College Miles goes to? Did I ever mention it? I was pretty confused while writing this so I randomly picked Pennsylvania lol.

Chapter 16 - The Truth Sometimes Hurts The Most

T ime will tell

Anxiety.

Every single muscle in my body felt extremely tight. My brain was screaming at me to go back home before it was too late, but my legs didn't want to move. I felt paralyzed. A lot of different thoughts were racing through my mind like crazy and each one drove me mad. He was going to be here any minute. I'd have to actually face him right now. There was no going back anymore.

I had no idea what I was expecting - or perhaps who I was expecting. My heart rate was accelerating each passing second and I had to grab my chest very tight to make it stop somehow. This felt like some sort of nightmare I couldn't escape from and I prayed to be woken up again. This situation felt overwhelming and I hated this feeling. The feeling of the unknown. The feeling of not knowing what to expect. The feeling of anxiety and fear.

My limbs tingled while my lungs were running out of breath as I kept walking back and forth in the diner Baldwin and Austin decided to meet. Although I briefly remembered what he looked like, I had no idea whether I could recognize or identify him, but the actual question was: did I even want to? No. I wanted to run back to my doorm, lock myself in there and do what I can do best: blame myself. I didn't want to encounter him, I really didn't. Why did he even agree to meet me? What does he want from me? How much does he actually know about me?

While my thoughts were driving me insane, I noticed that this place wasn't as crowded as I thought it would be. A few people were staring at me and shooting some weird glances my way since I was probably looking like a maniac to them due to my weird behavior, which caused me to sit down on one of the many empty seats right by the wall in the far corner. I couldn't stop tapping my right foot against the wooden floor though which was making a rather loud noise.

I took a short glance at my watch and back up to the door made of glass. He was twenty-two minutes late. I made a deal with myself: If he won't be here in less than a minute, I will get up and leave this place, but to my despair, the door swung open when I reached twenty-eight seconds.

A rather tall blond guy with a backpack rushed through the door and seemed to be out of breath once he came to a halt. He wasn't very muscular but still lean and fit. He had a thin face with a stern expression and a smooth, silky skin. His clothes didn't seem average but rather "rich", expensive and vintage. He drove a hand through his ash blond hair, which was neatly combed but his squiff still managed to look very untamed somehow.

His cheekbones were very present and he licked his lips as he pushed his eyebrows together while roaming around the room - until he spotted me. I probably looked like a deer caught in the headlights but I could definitely tell that he wasn't sure whether I was the person he was looking for since we both had never seen each other before.

It was him though, I could tell. What am I supposed to do now? Wave at him? Walk towards him and introduce myself? Or should I just remain seated and ignore him? I was completely overhelmed and confused. Fear crept its way into my brain again and I closed my eyes to escape from this cruel reality.

Man up now! Stop being scared and go confront him. Stop acting like a scared little boy, you're stronger than you think, my subconscious added and I took a deep breath in before I re-opened my eyes and gathered enough strength to finally put my hand up to signalize that I was indeed the person he agreed to meet with. His eyes were roaming around the room for a second time and when they finally landed on mine for a brief moment, we just stared at each other for a while until he nodded.

I raised myself from my seat very slowly as he took long strides towards my table. "Uh hey," he greeted, taking his bag off of his shoulders and placing it onto the floor underneath the table. "I'm Austin."

I nodded, "Miles." I introduced myself shortly as I reached my shaky hand out for him to shake but instead of making an effort to accept it, he just stared at my hand and rejected the hand shake a few seconds later, which caused me to take my hand back down and my anxiety to get worse.

"So, I honestly don't want to sit here and become best friends with you," he stated, leaning forward as he lifted his eyebrows in amusement and anger. "I'm also not here because you asked me to come," he continued. "I'm here because of Rose."

I avoided his gaze and stared at my shoes as I registered what he just told me. "Look—"

He held his hand out in front of my face which caused me to stop talking and rather look at him in surprise. "No, you look," he mocked. "Why are you back, Miles?"

Why am I back? This was a really good question. I balled my shaking hands into two fists to make it stop. I was sick of looking so weak because he seemed so cool and relaxed. I mean why was I the anxious one in the first place? Shouldn't he be scared that Rose might want me back? "I've always been here. Never been gone." Those were the only words I managed to say.

He smiled, shaking his head in amusement. "Never been gone? Are you serious? You have no freaking idea how hard I am currently trying to behave because the temptation to connect my beautiful fist with your jawline is very, very big."

"How much do you even know about me?" I asked, leaning forward as well this time to make him understand that I wasn't scared of him.

"Enough to despise you with everything I am." He nearly whispered while creating a bigger gap between us. "I'm not gonna sit here and talk about the past with you. I'm simply here to tell you face to face, man to man to keep your distance. Rose is happy - happier than she has ever been. She doesn't need you. She doesn't want you. She doesn't love you. She doesn't even care about you anymore. You're just a dark chapter from her past she finally managed to erase, so don't dare to walk back into her life. Stay away from her. You're nothing more than a strangerzm." He hit the table with his fist to create an impact but I just continued to stare at him with no emotion at all.

"Is she truly happy?" I asked, holding back my tears by not blinking although my eyes were burning.

"As I said: happier than she has ever been. You did this to yourself though, so I'm not going to pity you," he chuckled. "I'm begging you to stop contacting me from now on. I - or perhaps we - don't want to have anything to do with you. Don't be selfish for once in your life and do what's right. The next time I see your name somewhere, I won't be this gentle. Bye."

"Does she know that you're here right now?" I ignoried his previous statements again while trying to keep a straight and emotionless facial expression — which kept fading.

He rubbed his cheeks. "She doesn't. And it stays that way."

I inhaled a long and deep breath in as I covered my face with both of my hands since I was exhausted and defeated. He grabbed his fancy backpack and glanced at me briefly before he turned around to leave the diner but once he took a few steps forwards, he turned around to look at me again. "There's one more thing."

"Huh?"

"Here," he placed his backpack onto the wooden table in front of me and rummaged through it until he found what he was looking for: letters?

"What is this?" I wondered, taking those pieces of paper out of his hand to stare at them confused.

"Unaddressed letters to you."

"Unaddressed letters to me?" I repeated, pushing my eyebrows together in shock.

He nodded, "I want you to read them."

"Why?" I couldn't seem to understand why he would give those letters to me, but most importantly: did Rose know?

"Read them and you'll understand why."

"Does Rose know?" I asked, looking up at his tall figure from my seat.

Instead of responding to my question, he turned around and just left.

—

author's note:

OH MY GOD! How would you rate this chapter?! I'm so...unsure. I kinda like it but kinda don't? I wrote a chapter but it got deleted because my laptop decided to die before I had the chance to save the draft, so I had to write a new one (which sucked!).

I still hope you enjoyed this. If you did: PLEASE let me know! I really appreciate feedback and comments.

A vote (and a comment) are so, so appreciated.

Thank you & I love you.

Chapter 17 - Unaddressed Letters

T ime will tell

"You have a way of coming easily to meAnd when you take, you take the very best of meYou put up the walls and paint them all a shade of grayAnd I stood there loving you, and wished them all away."

—Cold As You, Taylor Swift

—

I couldn't bare to sit in that diner any longer when Austin left, so I jumped straight into my car and drove somewhere I could be all by myself: the French Creek State Park. I usually always end up at the beach at around midnight because no single soul could be found there, but during the afternoon the beach was crowded and I simply wanted to be left alone. And although the French Creek Park tends to be just as crowded as the beach at around this time, I had a secret spot where I couldn't be disturbed. The only sound that distracted me was the soothing sound of birds chirping. I honestly loved the sound of it so much that I fell in love with this place.

Once I parked my car close to the river and walked a couple of minutes into the forest, I sat down on a huge piece of branch that had fallen down from a tree sometime in the past. I closed my eyes briefly and just inhaled the fresh air that was surrounding me before I focused on the letters in my shaking hands. A voice inside of my head kept telling me not to read them, but I had to. I already knew that the content of these letters would hurt me, but I owed this to myself.

I took another minute to stare at the blue sky above while tapping my right leg into the mud out of nervosity. Now or never. "Let's do this," I whispered in front of myself as I opened the first one out of the four letters Austin handed me. I practically felt my heart slide down into my belly once I was confronted with her handwriting. I can't do this. I am scared — way too scared. I'm scared to face the truth, I whispered to myself. Yes you can. You don't just owe it to Rose, but to yourself as well. You have to be confronted with the truth, my subconscious added.

When I finished unfolding the white piece of paper slowly, I put my left hand onto my chest and tried to slow down my rapid breathing in an unsuccessful way. My heart was about to jump out of my chest as I was starting to feel my anxiety crawl back into my mind. Even my teeth were clacking, creating a very disturbing sound. I pushed my eyebrows together and began to read whatever she had to tell me.

September 22, 2016

Miles,

I feel like this is the fivehundreth letter I've been wanting to write to you within those past months. I have no idea where to start or how to put my damn thoughts and all the pain into words, but I need to express all of it. I want you to understand how you've damaged me. I don't care whether this sounds horrible, but I want you to feel just as miserable as I do. I want you to feel even worse.

My life has gone downhill the day I have met you and I'm still trying to understand - still trying to figure out - why I was the victim of this mess. Why did I deserve to feel like this? Why did I deserve to endure this pain? Why did my heart become the victim of your attacks? I have never not once done anything bad to you, but you still decided to harm me.

After all, I still wonder: Did I not mean anything to you? Not even once? I mean you asked me for my love and when I gave you my all, you pushed me around and cut me out of your life. I never meant to hurt you. I never meant to harm you or put you in any pain. All I ever wanted was to be happy. I wanted to be happy with you. I wanted to make you happy.

I failed.

I thought you were the best thing that ever happened to me, but you turned out to be the worst. You turned out to be a monster, a killer even. You wrapped me around your filthy fingers and damaged my brain. And if this wasn't enough, you killed me slowly. I'm not saying that all of this is your fault only, because I was too blinded by you. You manipulated me into thinking that I couldn't survive this life without you. You manipulated me into thinking that I needed you. You appeared in my life around a time I really needed someone and took advantage of all the messed up things that happened.

I always told myself that you would eventually change but you never did. I was an idiot because I actually believed in you — in us.

I guess the monster in me truly loved the monster in you.

—

My entire body was shaking after I finished reading the first letter that was addressed to me. My eyes were burning and I knew that once I blinked, those damn tears would flood down my cheeks. I let the piece of paper slip from between my fingers and covered my face with both of my hands instead. I sucked my bottom lip between my front teeth and began to cry uncontrollably loud. I was a bad person — such a bad person. I hated myself for everything I ever put her through. I hated myself for being the person I was. I hated myself for breaking and hurting her the way I did.

I couldn't cope with this. Each time I was confronted with my past, I felt this major pain in my chest that I couldn't get rid of and that hurt me so much. There was nothing I could to to change all the messed up things I did to her and that was the worst part of it all. She suffered so much because of me. How was I ever able to sleep peacefully at night again?

I rubbed my eyes and grabbed the second letter. I knew that her words would cut through me like a knife, but I deserved to suffer. I deserved to feel like this. These letters were her way of dealing with all of this mess. She never wanted me to read them, but I deserved to.

October 13, 2016

Miles,

how can a person be cold as you? I wasn't expecting you to call or reach out to me, but a flicker of hope inside of me made me believe that you would. Do you not wonder or care how I am feeling or doing after all the things you caused? It's 02:58am right now and all I can think of is how you broke my heart and humilated me in front of everyone. I somehow can't seem to move on from you. Why? I don't know. You gave me so, so many reasons to despise you, but I know that if you called me right now, I'd probably give you another chance — a chance you obviously don't deserve.

Why do I feel like my world is still revolving around you? Why do I feel like I can't breathe without you? You're not even worth any of my time.

I keep having nightmares about you. I keep waking up in the middle of the night just thinking of you. I cry myself to sleep every single night since you've left me standing in the cold, Miles. I can't keep up with this. I truly wonder how long I can endure this pain — how many more weeks or months, maybe even years. Although I need to save myself, I just can't. I'm way too weak to get over this, to get over you. I'm so lost in my own mind and thoughts that I can't find a way to get myself out of this.

I still ask myself how my life got to this point every single day, but I don't have the answer.

Sometimes, I can still feel your arms around me — still feel you around me. I can still smell your cologne and hear the way you laugh. And other times I can feel you forget me like I used to feel you breathe. It's strange to think that everything is gone now. And I know that after all these months, we can never be the same again. Our "love" - or perhaps my love for you - has been buried somewhere in the past and all that's left are those hurtful memories.

I guess we were built to fall apart from the very beginning.

There is one more thing before I can close this dark chapter once and for all:

Was ist worth it? Was she worth it?

—

"No," I cried to myself while wiping my tears with the back of my right hand. "She was not worth any of this, Rose. If only I could tell or show you how truly and utterly sorry I am for this... I know that I should have reached out to you, but I...I couldn't. I was a coward — scared to be confronted with the damn truth and scared to admit that I did you so dirty. I couldn't even man up and apologize to you. I could've solved this, but I simply chose to ignore it. I thought you needed space and distance. I wanted to give you enough time to get over this — get over the fact that I hurt you so deeply. I can see that it was a wrong desicion to let time solve this."

I had no idea how I was feeling now in this very moment, because there was so much I could have done to help her. She suffered for years even after we lost touch. I thought it would be better for the both of us to create some space, but turns out it wasn't. We both simply suffered separately. As selfish as it may sound, I really thought that she would eventually come back running to me once she realized that she still loved me even after everything I put her through.

I honestly just hate myself.

December 19, 2017

Miles,

why am I even still wasting my time by writing these letters to you? You won't ever get to read them anyway and I'll probably throw them away once I finish healing. But I guess I still put some effort and thoughts into this because it feels good to pretend that I am talking to you when you're so many states away from me. Even after two years, I was hoping that you would eventually return and beg for forgiveness but you proved me wrong again.

Well, you don't have to call me anymore because I won't pick up the phone. And even if you tell me that you're sorry after all this time, I won't believe you like I did before. I swear to you that I could've loved you for the rest of my life but you left me standing in the cold. You had me crawling for you so many times, but not anymore.

I was a damn fool — a fool for you. You used to shine so bright in my eyes, but I watched all of it fade away with the blink of an eye. When you showed me your true colors, I felt disgusted by myself. I felt disgusted by the fact that I gave you my all. I trusted you with my entire heart and soul. I gave you so much, but got nothing in return. Well, I mean I did get something in return: self-hatred, self-harm, an even lower self-esteem and pain. Lots and lots of pain.

You simply used me for your own benefit and that hurts the most.

November 5, 2018

Miles,

Another unaddressed letter to you. Lately, I've been wondering what you've been up to. How are you feeling? ~~hopefully miserable.~~ As much as I wish that you would feel miserable and bad, I somehow can't seem to be a cruel person like you. I somehow still hope that you're happy wherever you are in life right now. I hope that you managed to get rid of your demons and found someone who could show you how to love again. Wait — do I really? I honestly don't know, Miles, but I think I do. I used to hate you so much, but I guess I don't anymore. As weird as it may sound, I think I'm feeling no emotions towards you at all.

I've learned to let go of my past. I've learned to love again, to live again, to laugh again — and most importantly: to be happy again. I couldn't have done this without the right people by my side and that means the most to me. I managed to bury you behind. You're not in my mind anymore. I mean yes, there are times where life keeps reminding me about you, or about things you and I did or stuff you talked about, but other than that I am free.

I can't say that I'm clean or 100% over you, but I'm on my way to get better. There is this guy that I kind of...like!? He definitely plays a huge part in this. He managed to help me heal. He managed to erase you from my brain. He even helped me to get rid of these dark clouds that were surrounding me. Life is truly worth living, and I am finally convinced that life indeed needs a bit of rain to create a beautiful rainbow.

I haven't written a letter to you for nearly a year, but last week there was a frat party and they were blasting Green Day real loud. I immediately thought of you and trust me when I tell you that the first thing I wanted to do was to write another letter to you.

Why? Because I actually managed to listen to 'Wake Me Up When September Ends' without crying while thinking about you and that was proof enough that I am ready to move on from you.

So I guess it's time to let go.

Farewell, Miles.

—

My heart was breaking. Literally breaking. She moved on from me. With Austin by her side she managed to get over our past and focus on their future. As I once said, she couldn't find the light she was desperately looking for within me, so she became the light.

Although she may think that Austin helped her to erase me off of her mind, I was damn sure that she managed to move on from me because she realized that I wouldn't return to her. And that was the sad part. All I had to do was to apologize and prove that I wasn't the stupid 17 year old Miles anymore. While feeling the worst I have ever felt before, I decided to drive back home to finally finish the damn letter I was desperately trying to write for the past three years.

I never knew how to or where to begin, but suddenly I felt as if I had so much to say. My thoughts were going crazy and I was excited to open up to her. I really had to get these thoughts and words out of my chest. I wanted to make sure that she knew how sorry I was and how much I had changed. I wanted her to understand that I managed to get rid of my demons as well.

...Dearest Rose,

I know that words aren't enough, but you are better than this...

[to be continued]

—

author's note:

Miles can finally write his letter!!! And I'm very excited to be back writing this story. Mayday Parade and T Swift are my source of inspiration for this and I truly can't wait to write the upcoming chapters because I think a lot of interesting things are going to happen.

If you're still here after all those months of my absence, I am sending a massive virtual hug your way.

A vote and a comment would mean so much to me!

THANK YOU.

Chapter 18 - And Another Fight

T ime will tell

Hits when I'm asleep right throughI'm cold when I wake cause I won't feel youWhen I can't breathe I know it's youGot a lump in my throat just thinking of you

—

I spent another couple of hours at the French Creek Park before I decided to drive back to my dorm. I didn't wear a jacket and after a while it just got way too cold sitting by the sea and I was in desperate need of warmth. I was hoping that Baldwin might already be asleep, but it was only half past eight and I knew that he would be waiting for me to return before he could go to sleep peacefully.

He was probably feeling guilty about agreeing to meet Austin behind my back — in my name. I didn't know whether I should make him feel extra bad about it because he stabbed me behind my back when he reached out to him and tried to fix things he couldn't fix at all. I mean I was aware of the fact that he just wanted to help me, but this was definitely not the type of help I needed or perhaps even wanted.

"Miles!" He nearly screamed when I unlocked the door, which caused me to roll my eyes. "There you are! Where have you been so long!? How has it been!? Was he nice?! Was he—"

"Baldwin," I cut him off straight away. "Drop it. I seriously don't want to talk about it." I walked over to my drawer and grabbed a sweater and some thick socks before I headed towards the bathroom to change. I mean there was nothing to talk about, was there? He came all the way here to tell me to stay away from Rose, which basically meant that he was scared.

He walked past me to block the entrance to the bathroom. "You're disappointed, I know and I am so beyond sorry Miles. I just... I never—"

"I said drop it, please. I want to change and fly home." I actually had to show up to classes this week, but I truly didn't feel like I could focus on any of that anyway. I wanted to see my father. I wanted to hug him and cry my heart out because I was hurt and in pain once again. My father was the only one who managed to make me feel like life was worth living and I was slowly losing hope and faith yet again, so I had to see him. My mind wasn't at its rightful place and he was the only person who could fix it.

"What?" Baldwin whispered, looking at me confused. "You are returning to Minnesota? Now?"

I nodded, trying to push him away but he was too stubborn and didn't move a slight bit. "Baldwin..."

"Miles, I want you to listen to me. I never had a friend. You are the first and only person who actually talks to me like I am worth something. You are the only person who volunteerely wants to look at me and listen to whatever I have to say — at least sometimes." He smiled shyly. "I don't know what true friendship actually is. This is the first time I'm calling someone my friend, although I seriously don't know whether I am allowed to even call you that. You tolerate me. You accept me for who I am. You don't judge me for the way I look or the way I talk and I'm really trying my best to give you back what you give me: happiness." I could honestly hear and feel his hurt when he said those words to me. Baldwin and I weren't as different as he always insisted. We were pretty similar. "This sound sappy and odd, but I genuinely want to help you. I want to help you reconnect with Rose. Now that I never tasted what friendship feels like, I am doing everything wrong, but I'm learning. If I could change the way I acted, I would definitely delete those messages and just... let time handle this. As you once said: only time will tell what the future holds."

I couldn't stop myself from forcing a smile because what he said truly meant a lot to me and as much as I tried not to admit it, Baldwin had definitely become the best friend I never had. "I appreciate your presence, my friend," I confirmed, squeezing his shoulder. "What's past is past now, so let's move past this, shall we?" Pun intended.

"But why are you going then? You have an important exam this week." He folded his arms in front of his chest and furrowed his eyebrows at me. I totally forgot about my exam and mentally slapped myself for doing so.

I shrugged, avoiding to face him. "I have to. I'll be back by Wednesday, I promise. And I... uhm studied already. It's an easy one anyway. Now let me walk past you," I demanded nicely.

He moved aside to make enough room for me to finally enter the bathroom as he gave in with a loud sigh. I was glad that he stopped asking any more questions or talking to me at all because I didn't feel like talking to anyone but my dad right now.

—

It was around midnight when my plane landed in Minnesota and I still couldn't stop thinking about Rose's letters. Just thinking about them put me in such a bad mood because they kept reminding me of the person I used to be. They kept reminding me of the cruel things I did to her and to all the other people around me who only wanted nothing but the best for me. But most importantly, those letters kept reminding me of the most beautiful girl I used to call mine. Now I was more determined than ever to finish my very own letter for her, although I had no idea how I could hand it to her once it was done.

I grabbed my small bag and walked through the airport entrance before I called an uber and asked him to drive me home. Coming back to Minnesota still made me feel some different type of way because so many beautiful and even a lot more horrible memories were linked with this city. I stared out of the foggy window and tried to count some stars that were shining bright tonight. My heart nearly dropped into my stomach when my sleepy eyes noticed the red and blue lights radiating from my neighborhood from afar.

Something has happened. I sat up straight and rolled the window down to get a better look at whatever was happening immediately. My first thought was that something bad had happened to my parents, but when I read the street sign, it said 'Grand Rapids Street'. We weren't living in that street, so I exhaled out loud and put my hands on my face to recover from this small shock. The closer we got to the crowd of people that had gathered around the ambulance, the more I recognized who this house belonged to. Mr. Redley was living here - he only lived less than a minute away from us.

I placed my cold hand on top of my heart to stop its rapid beating as I nearly whispered, "I'll drop out here, thanks." I handed the uber some money and jumped out straight away after I secured my bag around my left shoulder.

The sound of the sirens made me extremely sick and also hurt my eyes, but I tried my best to block those noises as I searched for my parents inbetween the crowd. Once I spotted my dad in his yellow jacket and black slippers, I rushed over to him in a hurry. "Dad, what happened here?" I asked, placing my hand on his broad shoulder.

He turned around to face me with bewilderment and shock written all over his pale face. "Miles!? What are you doing here?" He looked me up and down as he undressed his jacket to place it around my shoulders instead. "Aren't you cold, son? Where is your jacket?"

I smiled lightly. "I— I wanted to see you. But for now could you please tell me what's going on? Did something happen to Mr. Redley?"

He avoided to look me in the eyes as he shook his head slowly. "He had a heart seizure. They say he probably won't make it."

I turned around to face the ambulance again before I wiped the sudden tears in my eyes away. Mr. Redley was an elderly man, probably around eighty, with the most generous heart and the biggest smile. He was living in this house for fivty-something years, so I basically knew him ever since I was a baby. His wife passed away in September a couple of years ago and I could still remember how painful it was and ever since then, Mr. Redley stopped talking to people. He stayed home most of the time and just watered his plants every once in a while. His two daughters moved far away and didn't visit him often — or at all. His son and grandchildren already gave up on him when he had his first heart attack about three years ago. And then it hit me, Andrew and I used to visit this old man nearly every day after school until we suddenly stopped and...drifted apart.

My mum and a couple of other women from our neighborhood took good care of him ever since. Back when his wife was still alive, he always gave me some money to buy icecream and chocolate with my friends. He spent a lot of time in his garden during the afternoon and drank some cups of tea with his significant other during the evening. They were always sitting on the porch and called me whenever I walked past their house. I really loved their company, but back then I was just too young to understand what they were talking about most of the time.

"How old are you again, Miles?" Mr. Redley asked, adjusting his glasses.

I took a huge bite from the chocolate-chip cookie Mrs. Redley baked earlier as I said, "I just turned fifteen."

"Fifteen, huh? I think I had my first girlfriend at that age," he laughed, staring at the street opposite us. "I learned a lot of things at that age, but back when I was your age everything was so different."

"I'm not keen with love." I shrugged, finishing the delicious cookie before I grabbed another one. "My dad always says that too."

He laughed again, but his laughs turned into coughs straight away. I handed him a glass of water and he gulped it down as he said, "Love is the most beautiful thing out there. Once you get older and more mature, and once you get the taste of it, you'll never want to let go of this amazing feeling. I hope I'll still be around when you get married."

I could feel my cheeks heat up and turn a dark shade of pink when he said those words. "I hope so too," I whispered even though I had no idea what he was talking about and why he said that.

"Love is like a flower. Water it and it will grow into something very beautiful. But if you keep adding toxic things to it, it will rott sooner than you think. Be a gentleman. Take care of your woman. Worship her. Show her that you love her every single day. Make her happy."

"Harrison, stop annoying that poor boy with your blabbering," Mrs. Redley scolded nicely. "He's too young for this. You should probably talk about these kind of things in another five years, right Miles?"

I simply nodded and smiled at those two.

Sadly, this was our first and last dialogue about love because we never talked about it again and that upset me. I truly loved Mr. Redley but he had just been suffering for the past years. He deserved to be happy again and I knew that Mrs. Redley was waiting for him to finally come back home. She was waiting for him in heaven and I guess it was time for them to reunite again after being separated for nearly five years.

"What the hell are you doing here!?" I heard someone shout as I got pulled out of my thoughts. Within seconds, someone grabbed me by the collars of my sweater, causing my father's yellow jacket to fall onto the ground during the process.

I needed another second to figure out who I was facing because he looked so unfamiliar and different. "Mr. Johnson?"

He pushed me to the side while still holding onto my collar like his life was depending on it. "I said what the hell are you doing here?"

I spotted the circle that formed around us within just seconds and heard a few gasps before my father interfered. "Robert!" He shouted as he tried to unlock his tight grip on me. "Let go of him right now!"

Mr. Johnson was furious. He was spitting fire and his chest was rising and falling in such a fast pace that I was scared something might happen to him if he didn't calm down within the next couple of minutes. "Mr. Johnson..."

He closed his eyes briefly. "Why are you even here? Didn't you move out and far away? How do you even dare to come back after all the dirty and unhuman things you did to my poor daughter?" His voice was so loud that I felt more than just embarrassed in front of our neighborhood. He definitely had every right to say whatever he wanted to say to me right now because I deserved it.

"Robert..." My father put his arm around his shoulders to calm him, but he jerked away.

"Don't you even dare to protect this... this... monster! To even believe that I allowed him to stay at our place... I seriously hate myself for giving you the access to hurt my daughter the way you did. Do you know how awful it was for me to see all those scars on my daughters body? You ruined her. You ruined her life! To think that she could have done even worse things to herself makes me sick. You should be ashamed of yourself. You should be ashamed to even look into a mirror. You disgusting piece of—"

"Robert!" My father nearly screamed this time. He was looking angry now and moved forward to step between us to create some more distance. "I said stop it, right?"

I pushed my father aside gently, "Let him talk. Please keep talking Mr. Johnson."

Both of them looked confused, but the confusion on Mr. Johnson's face disappeared straight away. "I don't want to waste my breath on you. Rot in hell."

Those were his last words before he looked at my father and only shook his head in what seemed to be disappointment. I shifted my gaze down to the ground and bit onto my bottom lip to stop myself from crying out loud in anger for the second time today.

I guess I was destined to rot in hell after all.

—

author's note:

SORRY FOR ANY TYPOS! I didn't re-read the chapter.

BUT whey, the chapter 18 is here!!! Should we categorize this as a filler chapter? I don't know, but I have a lot of great things planned for the upcoming updates and we just can't around these type of chapter. *sigh*

I still hope you enjoyed this update and if you did, please don't forget to leave a comment down below and also vote before you leave.

Thank you from the bottom of my heart. <3

Chapter 19 - A Surprising Apology

T ime will tell

"Luck of the draw only draws the unluckyAnd so I became the butt of the jokeI wounded the good and I trusted the wickedClearin' the air, I breathed in the smoke."

Daylight, Taylor Swift

—

Two days had past since I returned home. Two days had past since Mr. Redley had a heart seizure. And it had also already been two days since Mr. Johnson told me to basically get the hell out of this town — and that's what I was about to do because it was time for me to get back to Pennsylvania. I barely slept for the past couple of days because, but what's new? Per usual my thoughts were keeping me up at night and once again, I kept tossing and turning in bed until I got so mad that I threw my pillow against the door. Those damn thoughts simply didn't allow me to rest and it was getting the best of me since I felt very weak and extremely exhausted now.

"Miles?" My father called out before he opened the door to my room slowly. "Hey."

"Morning," I responded, rubbing the dark blue circles under my sleepy eyes.

"You sure you want to come, right?" He asked, leaning his head against the doorframe. "He'll be happy to see you."

I nodded my head. "I definitely want to come, dad. Maybe this will be the last time I can ever talk to him again... I would never forgive myself if I didn't visit him today."

He smiled. "Alright. Be downstairs once you're ready." Before he had the chance to close the door, he looked up at me again. "Are you hungry? I've made some pancakes since your mom left early to go to the hospital with Kimberly to take care of Mr. Redley before all the visitors arrive. They may not taste as good as your mom's, but they're still eatable if you add lots of maple syrup."

I shook my head this time, hiding my laughter. "Thank you dad. I appreciate your effort, but no. I'm not hungry."

When he disappeared from the doorframe, I yawned and moved towards my old wardrobe to chang my clothes. I had to mentally prepare myself to be confronted with Mr. Johnson again if he decided to visit Mr. Redley in the hospital as well. I couldn't describe the feelings inside of me, but they were a mixture of fear and determination somehow. Sadly, the fear was eating me alive and there was not a single thing I could do about it other than allow it to destroy me from deep down within me.

...

Thankfully the hospital wasn't as crowded as I thought it would be. Other than my dad and I there were about three other people who came all the way to check on Mr. Redley. And to my surprise, they were about to leave when we entered this old building. A young lady at the reception provided us with some information about Mr. Redley's current state and his whereabouts. About a minute later, my dad knocked on the door one of the nurses guided us to and once a female voice responded, he opened the large door that separated us. "Hello Kimberly."

"Oh hello Brent," she greeted friendly and once she spotted me behind my father, she walked towards me with open arms. "Oh wow, hello handsome." I couldn't stop myself from smiling at her comment as I opened my arms to embrace her in a hug. "You're all grown up, Miles."

Although her son and I weren't on good terms, I always had a soft spot for his mother. "You're not looking bad yourself," I teased, adjusting my sweater. She laughed out loud before she put her right hand on top of her mouth to silence herself and looked behind to check whether she woke up Mr. Redley.

"Crazy how fast our kids grow, Brent." She looked quite shocked and my father nodded, looking at me with a proud expression on his face. "When Andrew came home a couple of months ago, I barely recognized him. He grew a beard, which looked awful," she giggled. "I forced him to cut it and thank God he did. He's just... a man now and I guess I don't want to accept that. For me he'll always be my little baby boy, right Lauren?"

My mom walked into the room as well, holding a large glass of water in her hand. "What?" she smiled, looking at all three of us.

"I said our kids will always remain five year olds in our eyes, right?"

She made a sad face at first, but her beautiful smile returned straight away. "Definitely. Miles may be 23 years old now, but trust me when I tell you that each time I look at him, I look into the eyes of the same six year old boy who always begged me or Brent to sleep in his bed with him because he was way too scared of the monsters under it."

I felt my cheeks turn into a deep shade of pink. "Mom..."

All three of them laughed out loud, while my gaze was glued on Mr. Redley's peaceful body lying on the hospital bed right by the window. Even from afar, I could see that his chest was slowly rising and falling, which made me happy. "Uhm... can I... can I talk to him?"

Kimberly nodded, "Of course you can, but he's asleep right now. Maybe we should wait outside until he wakes up. Is that okay, Miles?"

"I'm awake," Mr. Redley coughed out loud. My mom rushed over to him and helped him to gulp down some water from the glass she was holding in her hand. My dad looked very concerned, but when Mr. Redley held his hand up and asured that he was fine, his facial expression softened a slight bit. "Come here," he said looking at me.

"Me?" I wondered, looking over to my dad, who nodded.

"Go talk to him, Miles. We'll be outside." Kimberly, my mother and father all walked out of the room and closed the door. It took me some time before I finally gathered some strength to move my feet towards his bed.

Once I sat down onto the wooden chair by his bed, he lifted one of his weak arms and put his hand on my left cheek. "Miles?"

"Can you remember me?"

I could see how exhausting it was for him to move his body, let alone how much effort it took him to even open his mouth just to talk to me and I felt bad for practically making him talk to me. "Of course I can remember you. You grew up in front of my very own eyes, didn't you? My wife always gave you some bandaids. You loved the ones with the spider-motives on."

Listening to him somehow brought some tears to my eyes. "I probably still do," I joked. It was odd, because as he was talking, the memories were present in my mind already. I could remember the exact day I was trying to drive my skateboard but failed miserably. I probably cried for like five minutes until Mrs. Redley came running towards me with some bandaids in her hands. To soothe me and make me forget about the pain in my leg, she held out a few of those bandaids and asked which one I liked most — I responded by pointing at the one with the spider-motive on.

"How is your life going, Miles? I think the last time I saw you, you were about a head shorter and did not have a beard." He coughed uncontrollably again, but when I wanted to jump up and get some help, he grabbed my arm tightly and forced me to remain seated instead. "It's okay, I'm okay."

I adjusted myself and decided to answer his question. "It's... going. Life keeps going, Mr. Redley. It doesn't ask us how we're doing — we have to make sure that we're moving just as fast, which is quite hard sometimes."

"What is it... what burden are you carrying with you? What bugs you?" He looked serious this time. "It's quite easy to see through you."

I scoffed, rubbing my face. "I wish I could tell you. I don't even know how... or even where to begin. It's a long story. About a girl... who I've hurt. And now I'm kind of dealing with the aftermath of it." I played with my thumbs and hoped that we would talk about something else instead because I was definitely not in the mood to talk about my past.

"Do you love her?" he asked hoarsely. I could feel his voice get thiner, so I reached over and handed him some more water.

"Yes, I do." I whispered more to myself than to him.

"Truly love her?" he asked again.

I nodded, "Definitely."

"Does she love you?"

"I honestly don't know, but from what I've read, she hates me or perhaps dislikes me on a high level and I'm not even blaming her for feeling like that towards me," I replied truthfully. I could feel the pain in my chest rising again. The knife was twisting and turning in a cruel way.

"Hate is an emotion as well," he said, grabbing my hand in his.

"Yeah, but it's the wrong emotion, don't you think?" I was confused because I had no idea where this conversation was going. Maybe I should just leave and let him sleep.

"It's not hard to turn hate into love again. Apologize. Let your heart speak, Miles. Don't think too much. Grab a pen or a... a mobile phone of whatever it is you people communicate with nowadays and tell her how you feel deep down inside. Don't hide your feelings. You feel miserable? Tell her. You feel lost? Tell her. You feel like giving up? Tell her?" He managed to lift his upper body with all the energy left in his fragile body only to stare deep into my eyes. "You love her? Tell her!" He said louder.

Right as I was about to respond, someone interrupted our conversation by entering the room. We both averted our gaze towards the direction of the door and once the person finally revealed himself, I could feel my stomach turn after I recognized who he is. I let go of Mr. Redley's hand and just stared at Andrew with my mouth wide open. I probably looked like I had just seen a ghost. My brain was not functioning clearly and I didn't really know what to do. I was shocked and confused as hell.

Andrew was just as surprised to see me. His gaze was constantly shifting between Mr. Redley and I as he gulped. Damn did he look different — but somehow still the same. "Hey," was all he managed to say until it was my turn to respond. His face definitely remained the same. No beard, no mustache, no piercings or whatever. The only thing he changed about himself were his haircut and his clothes. He was wearing a beige cashmere turtleneck sweater with a brown coat combined with some dark chino trousers and expensive looking leather chelsea boots. Back in highschool, we laughed about people who dressed up like this, but I had to admit that he was able to pull this look off.

"Hey," I replied, slowly rising from my seat. My hands were quite sweaty, so I rubbed them together to get rid of the sweat and calm myself down. This was so weird. It was obvious that the two of us were overwhelmed by this encounter and had no idea what to do. Should we go in and hug? Fight? Talk like grown-ups? Ignore each other? Should I walk out and let them talk on their own?

"Andrew, why are you standing there like that? Come here!" Mr. Redley ordered, trying his best to get up from his hospital bed but both Andrew and I forced him to lie back down. "I thought you wouldn't come."

Andrew was just standing a few inches away from me now, but I didn't feel the urge to fight him or even ignore him. I somehow wanted to talk to him. I wanted to apologize and tell him how truly sorry I was for all the things I caused. I wanted to apologize for being an absolute asshole towards him. I couldn't really describe it, but deep down inside, I was more than happy to see him here right now because there was a lot I had to get off my chest.

"My mother told me. I had to come," he assured, hugging Mr. Redley like he was his very own grandfather. I mean he sort of was. Andrew was over at Mr. Redley's house most of the time when we were kids and even teens. Their bond was definitely stronger than the bond between Mr. Redley and his actual biological grandchildren. He loved Andrew quite a lot. For Andrew, Mr. Redley was also some sort of grandpa-replacement since his grandfather died when he was just a toddler.

Suddenly, Mr. Redley started to cry. His hands were shaking like crazy — I could see and feel it once he grabbed Andrew's left and my right hand in his again. This scene brought some tears to my eyes as well. "To see the two of you for one last time before I leave is the best gift for me. To see how far you both have come in life... I'm so proud of you two. Andrew," he said, looking at him. "You will become the greatest lawyer of this generation. You will be successful and so happy in life, I promise you. Keep on making us proud, son. I'll tell your father about you in heaven."

I looked over at Andrew, he was obviously close to crying as well, but I knew him well enough. He was holding back his tears to seem strong in fron of him, but he wasn't. I put my guard down long ago as I started to sob. "And Miles son," he coughed, staring deep into my eyes now. "You will get out of this dark bubble you're stuck in and once you're out, you'll realize that this life doesn't consist of black and white. It offers thousands of colors. Stop being so hard on yourself. You're so young. You still have your whole life ahead of you. As long as you both got each other, life can't harm you. Make sure to always be there for one another, alright?"

I felt ashamed. He didn't know about any of the events that occured. Andrew and I lost touch long time ago. I turned my back on him and tried to ruin his life because of a girl. I betrayed him for no reason at all. When I looked over at him Andrew, he was already looking at me. To look into his eyes and see all the hurt I've caused made me hate myself more.

A nurse walked into the room and disturbed our conversation. "Could you please walk out now? He has to take his medicine and rest."

We didn't want to leave him just yet, but we knew we had to. He looked exhausted and his face was very pale. I didn't want to force him to talk to us anymore. "We'll be back tomorrow, we promise." I spoke for the two of us as we headed outside. When I turned around one last time before leaving, he smiled up at me. I'll never forget that smile, that's for sure.

We didn't just walk out of his room, but out of the hospital as well. He walked in front of me and I followed right behind. When we entered the elevator, neither of us said a single word. Once outside, he sat down onto a bench right by the entrance and I did the same. We remained silent for quite a while until I wiped the tears from the corners of my eyes. "Andrew?"

He didn't move or look at me. Instead, he kept remaining silent. He seemed to be in deep thought. "I'm sorry, Miles."

—

...

author's note:

I AM SORRY FOR ANY TYPOS OR SENTENCES THAT DON'T MAKE ANY SENSE AT ALL.

HOLY CRAP. ALL TOO WELL HAS REACHED A MILLION READS!?!??!?!?! I am going absolutely INSANE because of this!?!?!? I definitely shed a few tears because this is a dream come true. I would have never in my life imagined to write a story with such an impact. I am - and will forever be - so, SO grateful for all of you. You guys have no idea how much this actually means to me. I wish I could give each and every one of you a hug. I don't even know what to say or what to write because I'm just so... shocked and happy at the same time. I owe it all to you. I love you peeps so much. I'm so happy that you stumbled upon that story and decided to stay once you read it. I wouldn't be sitting in front of my computer and keep writing this story if it wasn't for every single one of you.

The next chapter is already in the making!!!! I feel so inspired and happy now.

Thank you from the bottom of my tiny heart for your support.

A vote and a comment would mean the world to me.

— who's happy about Andrew's return!? I have to admit that I am, hah! :-)

Much love. <3

Chapter 20 - Andrew's Confession

T ime will tell

—

I shot my head up to look at him in utter surprise. "What?" I wondered, "No, no, no. I am sorry, Andrew. I am the head of all of this mess. It's weird isn't it? As much as we try to run away from our past, it keeps chasing us. No matter how fast we run, this city holds all the memories we try to burry so hopelessly and each time we return, it confronts us with our mistakes. I've done so much wrong in my life. I've hurt so many people... my parents, my friends, you... her..." I whispered, biting onto my inner cheeks.

He scoffed, shaking his head. "You're not the only one with a long list of mistakes, Miles. Look at me. I'm part of this mess just like you are. I've moved away from this city, from the people and from all the bad things that surrounded me here, but you're right. How long can we keep running? Because I'm out of breath, Miles. I'm exhausted. You were haunting me. I felt so bad for all the shit I put you through. I betrayed you. I was a coward and couldn't admit it to you or to Rose. If there's anyone who needs to aplogize...it's me."

"Let's admit that we both did bad things to each other. We both betrayed each other. We both hurt innocent people. Back then I thought I had every right to act the way I did, but I was just a complete idiot for thinking that way. Now that I'm older, I feel ashamed by myself. You have no idea how painful all of this is. I... I can't sleep at night, don't want to eat, don't want to take care of myself... I just want to disappear once and for all. The remorse is killing me, Andrew." I sobbed, hiding my face behind my shaky hands.

I felt him pat my shoulder lightly. "Whether you believe it or not, I understand and feel you. I suffered a lot because of everything that happened, trust me I did, but I've learned to move on."

"Can you... can you just tell me why? Why did you betray me? Why didn't you tell me about this thing between Jo and yourself? We were like brothers, Andrew. Why did you hide that from me? I was extremely disappointed because I would've done anything for you. You were the last person I'd ever expect to do such a cruel thing to me, so tell me why?" I asked. These questions were bugging me for over three years and I definitely needed answers. "I'm begging you to tell me the truth."

He let out a loud and long breath before he nodded, "I'll tell you the whole truth. I just wish you would have heard me out back then... at the party when I told—no begged—you to listen to me, Miles. Maybe things would have turned out differently then, but let's leave the past where it belongs, shall we?"

I rubbed my neck slowly, "I know and I feel truly sorry for all the pain I caused you... from the bottom of my heart."

"It's alright, mate. I don't want to say that you had the right to act that way, but you had a reason to be angry at me and since I've known you since we were toddlers, I should have known that once you found out, you'd kill me." A sad smile curved his lips. I looked away because I honestly didn't know how to apologize properly for my actions. I hurt him quite a lot and felt beyond sorry for it, but couldn't find the right words to tell him. The images of his broken nose, all the blood and his unconscious body were floading right in front of my eyes. I looked down at my knuckles and closed my eyes for a brief moment.

"Please just tell me," I begged with fear lacing on my voice. I had a very bad feeling about what he was going to tell me, so I prepared myself for the worst.

After a few seconds of silence, he began to talk. "Josephine and I never really had deep conversations. We only greeted each other whenever we stumbled upon each other on the streets or the grocery store or somewhere else. The only thing we ever had in common was the fact that she was living in my neighborhood and that she was dating one of my best friends... you. I didn't know much about her. I mean you told me a few things every once in a while, but other than that, she was a stranger to me." He paused briefly. "One night... after I came home from a football game, she was sitting on the steps to her porch. She was sobbing. I could hear her cries even from afar. Looking at it now, I wish I would have ignored it, but I sadly didn't, because my mom didn't raise me like that and I felt bad for her. I thought something happened between the two of you, so I walked up to her and sat down onto the spot right next to her. She didn't notice my presence at first, so I asked her about the reason behind her tears, why she was crying and whether everything was alright. For a split second she stopped crying and removed her hands from her face to look at me. She seemed very surprised when our eyes connected, but I could somehow tell that she was sort of... happy? to see me. She looked into my eyes so deeply and asked, "Do you really care? Do you really care why I'm crying or perhaps how I'm doing?" and although I was sort of confused, I nodded because well, I mean I did care. I wanted to know whether I could maybe help her out in any way. And then she dropped the bomb. Out of a sudden, she told me everything, Miles. She literally told me everything about you and about your relationship. She told me that she felt like someone who was only living to... please you? Like some sort of robot. I could see and tell how truly sad she was. Her tears didn't stop running down her cheeks the whole time we were talking."

I wanted to say something, but decided to remain silent until he was done talking.

"I didn't expect her to go into the details, but she did. She told me about the amount of sex you both had on a single day. She said that you two never had any deep conversations about life or the universe. She complained that you only talked about yourself and your problems at home and didn't really care about her life as much as she cared about yours. She said you never listened to her problems or her difficulties and struggles in life. She also admitted that she didn't feel loved by you. You told her that you loved her a lot, but apparently you never managed to prove it to her and that was the biggest problem for her. It was eating her alive. She was anxious —kinda scared— to lose you. She was hopeless. She didn't know what to do or how to escape from that relationship because you captured a huge part of her life and she simply didn't know how to live it without you. She was attached to you — way too attached to just let go. She was not only used to you, but that life she was sharing and living with you as well. Yet she hated that relationship because of how it made her feel — worthless. She wanted to feel loved though, truly and deeply loved by a man who could cherish her. I could really see how hard it was for her to openly talk about this — especially with me, a stranger. But I gladly listened to her talk about her problems and she appreciated that so much and then this..." he didn't know how to put it right. He kept searching for the word with his eyes as he pushed his eyebrows together. "This turned into some sort of routine. I offered my help without any bad intentions at all and instead of gratefuly taking my hand, she took my arm for granted and dragged me into this mess with her."

"Wh—" I wanted to ask something, but he silenced me with his index finger while avoiding to look into my direction. I was utterly confused. I cherished Josephine with everything I am or perhaps was. I loved her so deeply and I always made sure to make her feel the love I had for her. This was really making me question so many things in life right now. Back then I always thought that she was my soulmate, but like Andrew mentioned before, she also was a complete stranger to me. Who was this girl?

"I'm not done yet. During every conversation we had ever since that day, I realized that all she needed was someone to care about her and listen to her. But suddenly, things got weird. After another football game of mine, we gathered at Joey's diner to celebrate our victory. You know how much I hate to get drunk, so I walked straight home after finishing my first beer and dropping Rose off at home. Besides, I remember feeling extremely tired that night. So once I arrived home and walked the stairs up to my room, I nearly got a heart attack. Jo was sitting on my bed — I noticed her when I turned the lights on. At first I thought I was hallucinating, but when she walked over to where I was standing and grabbed my hand, I realized that she was in fact in my room and standing in front of me wearing one of my damn sweaters. When I asked her how she got here, she said that my mom let her in and due to my half-drunken state I... shrugged it off. I thought she was here to talk again, like we used to — turns out she had other things in mind and that's also where it sort of 'began'. She started to get undressed and that made me feel so uncomfortable," he emphasized strongly. "I mean I was still dating Rose at that time and I dropped her off at home like.... twenty minutes before this happend and I... I couldn't do that to her or to you. She moved closer and really unexpectedly, pressed her lips against mine and I let her do that. I kissed her back and this went on for about twenty seconds until my brain was sending me the signal to make it stop. I remember pushing her away from me a bit too harsh but I was shocked. I didn't expect her to kiss me... let alone think about sleeping with me when she was still dating you? I felt so freaking disgusted by myself. I kept rubbing my lips to get rid of her taste until my lips got swollen. I remember shouting at her and telling her to never do that again. Then she ran off crying, but I could've cared less. We didn't see or hear from each other for about five weeks after that awful incident. I kinda thought that you two managed to get past those problems — until she decided to call me up once again to apologize for her actions. I accepted her apology and well, we ended up talking about her issues like we were used to. That conversation felt like the very first we had. She kept complaining about your relationship, kept telling me about how you neglect her, about how you keep getting drunk and into fights and so on. My advice was still the same though: I told her to talk to you. I even offered to talk to you if she didn't want to, but she paniced and said, "No, no, please don't. I'm too scared to lose him. I think that's just how he is. This is something between him and I. I need to solve this. Don't get involved." — and so I didn't, which was a pretty dumb mistake by me."

I felt the familiar salty tears in the corners of my eyes. They were still present and I let them escape because there was no reason in holding them in. I had been living in a complete lie the whole time when I was dating her. Everything started to make sense to me now. I could connect the dots and count one plus one together. I finally knew the reason behind her mood swings and why she was acting weird and suspicious towards me sometimes. Andrew didn't say anything for about two minutes until he collected his thoughts and continued.

"It kept going like this for quite some time. She called me, we met, she talked and I listened. She called me, we met, she talked and I listened. She called me, we met, she talked and I listened. We did this for about four months? Maybe more, maybe less. I know I should have told you, I swear I do, but please don't ask me why I didn't because I don't have the answer. There was another time she tried to put her lips on mine, but like the first time, I rejected her and she apologized— straight away this time. She also begged me not to tell you and that should've been alarming for me. On that day, I understood that she wanted more from me. She didn't just want me to be the guy who listens to her problems. She wanted me to be the guy who pulled her out of that mess. She wanted me to be the one who saves her in some poetic way, but she had to save herself. And to my surprise, she admitted that she loved me a few days later. She looked me in the eye with tears in her own and begged me to take her. She begged me to stay over at her place and make her forget about you. And that's when I drew the line and told her to stop contacting me. She had to confront you with that. She had to be faithful and tell you about her feelings towards me, but turns out she never did. We stopped seeing each other again for a month or so until our paths crossed at Toby's birthday party. I broke up with Rose the night before because I cheated and then the whole Mandy incident was kind of spreading around and... I was feeling guilty. I wanted to punsh myself in the face over and over again because of what I did to an innocent girl. Even up to this date, I hate myself for it. For everything. I could have prevented this..."

The irony of this? I was feeling the exact same way like he did. His and my situation were quite similar, nearly the same even. I could exactly understand how he was feeling, just like he could understand how bad I was feeling about myself. We were going through the same type of pain separately and it was soothing to know that I wasn't the only one who had to suffer like this.

"I ignored Josephine the whole night. She wanted to talk to me when I headed towards the restroom, but I didn't let her speak. I seriously didn't want to have anything to do with her anymore. We had a small fight and I kept shouting at her because I thought that she ruined my life although I ruined it myself. I don't remember the exact time, but I think at around midnight, she texted me. She was drunk and threatened to harm herself. I called her. She didn't pick up at first, but after my third attempt, she picked up the phone and said that she was going to do something to herself. I tried to make her forget about her dark thoughts by saying some nice things about her. She didn't listen though. She cried and hung up the phone instead. I rushed over to you and told you to go and find Josephine before it was too late, but you were so drunk that you kept pushing me away, saying "Later, we'll talk later, Andrew." — You probably don't even remember me walking over to you, do you?" he asked and I shook my head, only to confirm that he was right. I was feeling beyond guilty.

"Thought so. You were trying to recover from all the alcohol you consumed, so I made my way through the house and tried to find her instead because I was actually scared that she might do something to herself. I ended up finding her in that room... the one you caught us in. She looked awful, Miles. She was sitting there on the cold floor with a damn knife in her right hand. Her mascara was mixed with her tears. Other than that she looked quite determined to actually do something to herself and she smelled like cigarettes. I was just glad that I got there in time. Although I was annoyed by her, I sat down to the ground and left a gap between us. I was close enough to grab the knife out of her hand to put it aside and far away from her reach. Then I asked her why she was feeling like this although I knew the answer already. She didn't look at me. The worst part of this? She turned out to be a great, great actress. She admitted that she didn't really plan on harming herself, she just wanted me to be close to her. She admitted that she couldn't bear to see me with other girls when she was the one destined for me. She told me about the moment she fell in love with me and how hard it was for her to accept the fact that I was in love with someone else. I didn't want to shout at her, so I tried my best to stay calm and talk to her in a nice way — in a way even she would understand that I did not have any feelings for her. Even then she didn't want to accept it. She simply didn't care. She had this sick obsession with me and while I was trying to process all of the information, I suddenly felt her against me. I was not drunk. I did have one beer and some whiskey, but I was definitely not drunk. Unlike me, she was completely wasted, but I'm pretty sure that she knew exactly what she was doing in that moment. She forcefully put her lips on mine and took her shirt off, but I previously told you to be honest, right? So yeah, I let her kiss me for a third time. Why? Because I was having this deep conversation with myself in my head while it happened - I didn't kiss her back though! Sadly, my brain was frozen for a split second and when it was working clearly again, I pushed her off of me... and then my eyes connected with yours. You know the rest of the story, don't you? Or do you want me to recap that part?"

Neither did I answer his question, nor did I move. I was digging my nails deep into my palm to sort of relax and stop myself from exploding. My eyes were freaking burning because I didn't blink for about two minutes. My eyes were fixiated on the trashcan by the entrance. It was a huge relief to finally know the truth behind the everything. A huge burden had been lifted off of me, but it didn't mean that it didn't hurt, because damn, it did hurt so badly.

"I want you to know that I never had any feelings for her. I never wanted this, never wanted to see you hurt. It may seem or sound like it, but I swear to you I never meant to hurt you like that. I was so dumb, so freaking dumb. I basically kissed your girlfriend behind your back. I kissed her without a reason. I- I made her cheat on you with me just like I made myself cheat on my own girlfriend with her. I wanted to tell you about it, trust me I did but I was so freaking scared. I was scared because I knew what you were capable of and I was aware of the fact how much you loved her. I didn't want to lose our brotherhood, didn't want to let our memories go to waste... my actions cannot be justified and what I did was absolutely wrong and not acceptable, but I definitely got what I deserved. And the one thing that makes me regret this even more is Rose because she was innocent. She had nothing to do with any of this. Yet you made her pay for my sins. I swear to God," he finally sobbed now, "I would have told you and I would have told her if I had known about your plans, about your revenge and about your true intentions. I would have said, "Hey Rose, listen, I cheated on you. I kissed another girl behind your back. Please be cautious if Miles enters your life", but I guess I didn't think that you would be that ruthless and cruel. I didn't think you were that heartless and would do such a horrible thing to her. I take full responsibility for everything that happened to Rose and that really kills me from deep down inside."

I wasn't sure whether it was my time to talk now because I seriously didn't know what to say or how to react to his confession since I was still stuck trying to process all of this. "Why did you sleep with Mandy?" Was the only question that came out of my mouth.

He bit down onto his lower lip, "Are you going to believe me when I tell you I never did?"

My head shot side-ways to look at him in shock and disbelief. "What!?"

"It was not really a big secret that she had a crush on me, right? I mean you kept making fun of it, remember? And well...since I was a coward and couldn't admit to you what the actual reason behind our breakup was, I told you a lie. I mean I was aware of that rumor of Mandy and myself and that a few people thought that we had one-night-stand, so yeah I basically lied to you about it, but I never in my life even touched her," he admitted, "I swear."

I rubbed my eyes and let out another loud and long breath I was holding inside for quite some time now. "I have no idea how to cope with all of the things you just confessed to me, Andrew. I was really living in a big bubble that was made of lies and lies only, but now since the truth is out, the bubble has been errupted and I'm falling onto the cold hard ground without a parachute."

"I'm sorry," he whispered.

"I need some time to process this. I'm grateful for your honesty, Andrew. I..."

"Miles!" My father shouted as he stepped out from the hospital, interrupting our conversation that was long overdue. "Mi—" he turned to his left and right and once he spotted us, sitting at the bench to his right, he moved closer. "Here you both are... I... I don't know how to tell you guys, but..."

"What's wrong, Mr. Reese?" Andrew asked, panic and fear evident in his shaky voice.

"Mr. Redley has passed away."

—

author's note:

I AM SORRY FOR ANY TYPOS OR SENTENCES THAT DON'T MAKE ANY SENSE!!!

BOOM. I loved writing this chapter so much — I'm sorry that Andrew's parts were so long! I simply didn't know when and wherevto split them lol. But hey, Andrew and Miles are on their way to rebuild their friendship all thanks to Mr. Redley and I am so ready to write some more dialogues between these two.

TO CLEAR THINGS UP: Remember that one chapter in All Too Well, where Mandy basically humiliates Rose at a party and Matt comes to her rescue? After that, Matt says something along the lines of "she [Mandy] ruined the relationship of some girl... slept with her boyfriend..." - let's not forget that he was dating Elsa at that time and Elsa was one of Mandy's so called "friends" who she used for her popularity status. Mandy wanted to raise her reputation and become a slight bit more popular by lying and saying that she slept with her school's very own quarterback - which was Andrew. I'll write more about this in the upcoming chapters though, don't worry!

If you have any questions concerning Andrew's confessions, please ask them right here. I'll try to wash away all the confusion, hah! :-)

QOTD: Thoughts after this long chapter?

Don't forget to vote and to leave a comment before you leave. It's appreciated.

Thank you. <3

Chapter 21 - Rose's POV

T ime will tell

"Sometimes in the middle of the night I can feel you againAnd I just miss you and I just wish you were a better man..."

- Better Man, Taylor Swift

...

I had been lying in this bed with my eyes wide open for the past hour or so. I loved these type of mornings so much — the ones where his strong arms were wrapped around my upper body and his cute little snores filling my ears, the ones where neither of us were in a rush to get to work, the ones where we would probably stay in all day and watch some movies after we've had breakfast. Austin usually slept until around ten a.m, while I was already awake at eight, so I just took this little extra time to count all my blessings, think about life and analyze his imperfect, yet perfect features.

Like always, his arms were wrapped around my body so tightly that I could feel his breath on my neck. My back was pressed against his muscular chest and I slowly tried to untangle myself from his grip to turn myself around to face him. Once I was looking straight at his angelic face, a smile spread around my lips. He was only wearing his grey shorts while his upper body was uncovered. He always complained about the fact that it was just too hot to sleep in anything else other than in his countless collection of shorts while I was wearing his over-size sweaters instead. I placed my hand on his bare chest and began to draw random letters with my fingertips very carefully. His lips were parted slightly and the sun was shining right on his face because he forgot to close the curtains last night.

The golden color from the sun had a certain effect on his hair as it looked a lot blonder now. The smile on my face dropped once this beautiful image in front of me was replaced with another image from my past and I jerked away immediately, causing Austin to open his eyes with confusion and tiredness. "I'm sorry," I whispered, rubbing his cheeks softly. "I didn't want to wake you."

He rubbed his eyes with his right hand as he let out a loud yawn because he knew that it annoyed me whenever he yawned that loud, but he just smiled. "Good morning, babe."

I rolled my eyes at him playfully, "Good morning to you too, honey," I teased.

We both continued to stare into each others eyes before I bit onto my lower lip and tried not to laugh. "Are you alright?" He pulled me even closer towards him and I could feel the warmth radiating from his body as I placed a soft kiss onto his neck.

I nodded, leaving his question uncommented. I had a weird dream last night and ever since then, I couldn't fall back to sleep because I was scared that I would dream about it again. "You should get some more rest, I'm alright don't worry," I said.

"Well, you woke me upso I'll sleep if you sleep too." He pulled a strand of my brown hair behind my ear and slowly caressed my right cheek with his thumb. "You look tired."

"I'm not," I stated, although I slept for a total of four hours only. I stumbled upon one of my old boxes I stored in the attic last night - that's probably why I'm feeling like this right now. The box was filled with memories from my past and a couple of letters I didn't want to throw away. Those were letters I wrote for Miles. Unfortunately, I decided to read one of those letters last night because it had been over a year since I had written the last one and I simply wanted to know whether they still had this unknown and unexplainable effect on me. Apparently they did.

"Does it have anything to do with whatever you stumbled upon in the attic last night?" he asked as if he had just read my mind and I looked at him in shock before I shifted my gaze away immediately.

In order to avoid his questions, I rolled out of the bed and grabbed my bunny slippers to walk over to the bathroom and wash my face with cold water to get rid of these thoughts and everything revolving around the letter I had written. Austin didn't let me go though. He jumped right next to me and gently turned my head sideways to make me face him again. "You know that you can always talk to me, right? We have never kept things from each other, so I'm begging you to please tell me whatever you have on your mind."

He was right. We both have known each other for four years now and we've always openly talked about our problems - especially after I told him about my past and why I was so scared to trust people. I had the pleasure to call him my boyfriend for a little over a year now and I had never kept any secrets from him ever since then. "I had a dream...which included a person I don't want to talk about."

His jaw clenched and I could feel how his body tensed, so I grabbed his hand in mine to soothe him. "What was it about?" He asked with curiosity evident in his voice, although he tried to hide it. I smiled, trying to assure that there was no need for any jealousy at all.

I looked down onto the white fluffy carpet we bought a couple of weeks ago. "I don't recall... I think it was about a random moment from the past, but I really don't remember the details or anything else." This was obviously a lie because I remembered every single detail from the dream and I had to admit that it felt beyond real. I really thought I would wake up staring into Miles' eyes.

"That's it?" he looked confused but relieved at the same time.

I nodded slowly. "I mean I found a couple of letters I had written back in college and I read a few of them. I guess they caused me to dream about him, but well thankfully it was just a dream and not reality. Can we drop this topic now?"

He squeezed my hand tightly. "I'd also love to drop this topic now. Thank you for being honest with me, Rose. Should we go out for breakfast?"

"Sure, let me get ready first," I placed a kiss onto his plump lips and rushed over into the bathroom to take a quick shower. Once I turned the faucet on, the dream flashed right in front of my eyes and I closed them to simply get rid of these thoughts and images wandering around my head.

...

He intertwined our hands as we were sitting right by the ocean. "I love you, Rose Johnson."

"And I love you," I whispered loud enough for him to hear before I jumped up from my previous position to rush towards the waves. I could feel his presence right behind me before he grabbed my waist to turn me towards him again. Our feet were already touching the wet sand and I couldn't stop myself from smiling like a little child who had just gotten some icecream.

"Since it's our anniversary next week, I want to hijack you for the night if that's alright?" he moved closer towards me until his body was hovering over mine. "I take my question back. I'm definitely going to hijack you, whether you like it or not." His dimple popped out once he laughed and I grabbed his face in my hands to put my lips on his eagerly.

He leaned in for the kiss and when our lips connected, I could feel my heartbeat quicken and the butterflies in my stomach errupt. I loved this effect he had on me and I wondered whether he felt a certain type of way whenever he kissed me as well. I secured my arms around his neck to deepen the kiss and when his hands on my waist moved lower, I pushed him away gently to pull my white shirt over my head and dive into the ocean. I loved to tease him like this.

He let out a desperate groan as he did the same. He tossed his shoes aside and got rid of his grey hoodie and dark-washed jeans before he followed me into the ocean. When our bodies were covered in water, he secured his arms around me from behind and whispered, "Look at this beautiful sunset. It's beautiful, isn't it? I mean it's not even half as beautiful as you are because you're breathtaking, my love and nothing can compare to your beauty."

I nearly drowned in the water as I began to cough uncontrollably, clinging onto his body with my dear life. "Damn Miles, you nearly cosed me to drown," I stated, staring deep into his blue eyes as a small smile crept over my face. "When did you start getting so romantic?"

He continued to smile. "I thought I'd finally let my inner Shakespeare out for you, my lady." I couldn't stop myself from laughing out loud at him for trying to fake Shakespeare's british accent. I remember stumbling upon a few of Shakespeare's plays when I visited him in College and I also remember him indirectly admitting that he loved Shakespeare and his works once.

I chuckled, squeezing his cheeks. "You should let him out more often, my lord."

"I just might," he said. "My lady."

The beautiful orange shades from the sun were making his blue eyes look even more beautiful and I couldn't take my eyes off of him for the hundreth time today. "You're the best thing that happened to me. I'm glad that we still manage to see each other so often even during College. You have no idea how much this quality time means to me."

"I thought it was my part to say all these nice things to you? Stop making me blush, Rose. If I could show you how much I love you, I would. But it's impossible," he tried to look serious but his dimple popped out again, followed by his familiar smile. "Let me drive you back to your dorm, you have to study, remember?"

"I don't want to go to my dorm just yet," I complained with disappointment lacing on my voice. "We haven't seen each other for nearly a month. I've missed you so much. Let us spend some more time, please. I promise I don't even need much time to study."

"The sun is currently setting and you said you have to study for your exam tomorrow and since we've been hanging out for the past couple of hours, you didn't have the chance to study at all," he remarked and I rolled my eyes at him because we both knew he was right. "Don't pout! You know that's my weakness."

I continued to pout. "But you're staying with me tonight, right? My roommate is gone."

He licked his lips. "You and I both know that you wouldn't even get the chance to study if I stayed over."

"You wanna bet?" I challanged, throwing some water into his face.

"Rose..." he rubbed his face, grabbing my body from behind to place a kiss onto my neck.

I closed my eyes and let out a moan. "Miles?"

"Mhmm?"

"Please hijack me next week," I begged.

He laughed, kissing the soft spot under my earlobe passionately. "Don't even worry about it."

...

"Rose," Austin knocked on the door and I immediately unlocked it, rubbing the spot under my earlobe. "Are you ready?"

I nodded, rushing towards my wardrobe to grab a shirt and some jeans. "Just give me five more minutes."

"Are you sure that everything is alright?" He leaned against the doorframe with a worried facial expression. "I mean we can stay home and prepare some breakfast as well."

I scratched my neck this time. "I want to go out with you though. I'm sorry, I'll hurry."

He disappeared in the living room as I let out a loud breath I didn't even know I was holding. What's going on with me?

Once I made sure that Austin was gone, I walked over to my dresser and opened the second drawer to pick up the letter from last night. This short letter really messed with my head and I wondered why I had even written it. I mean in my dream Miles was in fact a better man, but after all it was just a dream. I had no idea who he was today - he was a complete stranger to me. Four years were a very long time, maybe he had changed...

Dear Miles,

I wish you were a better manI wonder what we would've becomeIf you were a better manWe might still be in loveIf you were a better manYou would've been the oneIf you were a better man

—

author's note:

Hi guys! MERRY CHRISTMAS!!! My small, little gift for you guys is this chapter. I know it's short and -welp- a bit boring but since this story doesn't really have many chapters left, I thought I'd add this filler because this chapter is only preparing us for what is going to happen *wink, wink* :-)

I hope you spend some amazing time with your family and loved ones.

If you happen to read this, please make sure to vote and maybe leave a nice comment down below.

Ps if you really want to get into the mood of this chapter, listen to "Better Man" by LittleBigTown (or perhaps T Swift).

Much love.

Chapter 22 - Hope

T ime will tell

I just want to be wanted I could use a little love sometimesI just need to be needed Like to know I'm crossin' someone's mindI just want to be someone that somebody needsI just want to be more than a drop in the sea

- Wanted, OneRepublic

—

I honestly didn't think or know that I would be this affected by death, but apparently I was very affected by it. Everyone's heads were down. Some people were crying, a couple of others weren't. I was part of the latter. I wasn't crying because I just knew that Mr. Redley didn't want me or perhaps anyone else to be sad about his passing, so I tried my best to be strong - or at least seem strong. Andrew was standing right next to me and his tears just didn't seem to stop dripping down his face ever since we arrived.

There was a picture of Mr. Redley right by the darkblue coffin and I truly tried my best to keep it all together, but that picture had a certain effect on me. I couldn't stop looking at it - at him. The way he smiled and all the happiness he was radiating on that picture...I could feel it. It was hard to explain it, but it seemed as if he was still here...standing somewhere in this church and looking at all of us. That picture seemed so real and so alive. I suddenly wondered what he looked like under that coffin. I had seen him a few days ago, but I wondered how much he had changed within that short time span.

My thoughts were interrupted by the preacher who began to read out passages and without actually realizing it, my eyes got wet. After the preacher was done, we continued to listen to some speeches from a couple of people on the makeshift stage. Andrew's mother was also one of the many people who walked up there to deliver a speech as well. I turned my head sideways to look at her son on my right and shot a sad smile his way before I squeezed Andrew's shoulder tightly.

She sobbed and her voice was thick, "Mr. Redley was a...very humble and generous man. I think he has touched all of our lives with his attitude, innocent heart and positive mindset. He loved to reach out his hand for people in need. He radiated such a joyful spirit and managed to turn sadness into happiness so effortlessly. He-" she paused, clearing her throat after she wiped away the tears with her white tissue from under her swollen eyes. "He has been such a support system for me over the years ever since I moved to this town. If it weren't for him, I would have never met the love of my life." She looked down at her husband, whom she married six years after Andrew's father passed away. Mr Redley introduced them to each other and well...the rest is history.

Due to the circumstances and her touching speech, a hot tear escaped from my eyes again.

"Mr. and Mrs. Redley didn't just support me but my son as well. They helped him and shaped him to be the man he is today. I owe them so much, so this loss is very heavy and my heart is hurting so much right now." She placed her shaking hand on top of her heart and closed her eyes for a brief moment. "You'll always be in my heart and mind forever," she said a few feet away from the microphone but we were still able to hear her before she walked down the stairs and sat down next to her husband and son.

"Beautifully said, Kimblery," I whispered over to her and she gave me the same sad smile I gave Andrew a few minutes ago. Instead of saying anything, she squeezed my hand and didn't let go of it afterwards, so I placed my other hand on top of it. This small gesture proved to me that Andrew and I were indeed more than just friends - we were brothers. His mother never separated the two of us, she was always so nice to me whenever I was over at their house and took care of me as if I was her own son as well. She really made me feel all the love she had for her son and that touched me.

When we all gathered around at the windswept graveyard and they lowered Mr. Redley's coffin into the hole they digged earlier, Kimberly let go of my hand and placed her arm around Andrew to hug him tightly. She pressed him against her chest and caressed his back slowly. Step by step all the men were taking the spade and began to cover the coffin in dirt...

And then he was gone forever.

-

"Hey, I was looking for you," I said as I sat down next to Andrew. He was sitting on a pew in this tiny church while he was looking at the high arched windows. I inhaled a long breath before I focused on the stained glasses surrounding us. "How are you feeling?"

It took some time until he noticed my presence and when he finally did, he turned his head sideways to look at me. "I'm happy that he is in a better place now."

I nodded in agreement, "So am I."

"Why were you looking for me?" He asked, leaning back as he folded his arms in front of his chest. I really wondered what was going through his head, but at the same time I didn't want to know. Even as kids, Andrew would always come to this church to think about life. He once told me that this holy place brought him tranquility, so I decided to stay here for a little longer because somehow, this place had the power to tame the spirits in my head.

"I wanted to say goodbye," I informed. "It's time for me to fly back to Pennsylvania."

"College?" He asked and when I turned my head to look at him, I noticed that he was staring at the candle holder in front of us.

"Yeah...I've been absent for quite a while now and I'm already behind with all this stuff. I should've already graduated half a year ago, but I just can't focus on my degree," I admitted truthfully. I had a lot of things in mind which kept me from gathering enough motivation to study - let alone to pass my exams. I skipped most of them and from the looks of it, I had to skip them again.

"Oh, why?" This time he was looking straight into my eyes and I was the one who looked away because I honestly didn't want to talk about it. I was sick of myself for constantly bringing up the same topic: Rose. I was sick of complaining about how miserable I've been ever since she left because I was going in circles and it only made me dizzy.

"It's so freaking hard to simply live, Andrew. I've got demons and they won't let me rest, won't let me sleep, won't let me move forward," I mumbled in front of me.

He exhaled out loud. "I'm so sorry. I know how you keep struggling with all these mental health problems, I should've reached out for you. No matter how bad we both hurt each other, you're my brother and I should've taken care of you. Why don't you get some help? Maybe visit a therapist?"

I shook my head, knitting my eyebrows. "I need to deal with this on my own. I deserve it, you know? If I would get professional help, it would be too easy."

"You deserve it?" His voice sounded a mixture of angry and confused. "You are torturing yourself, are you aware of that? You were a dumb eighteen year old teenager with a hard life. I mean you've always been a rebel and when you started hanging out with the wrong crowd and let your guard down, it was easy to see through you. You were surrounded by fake people - apparently me included. I can really see how much you've changed. You've turned into the likable fourteen year old Miles again." He genuinely smiled at me and I appreciated his honesty. "Now stop being so hard on yourself."

I scoffed, "Well maybe I should've used my brain? Come on Andrew, let's be honest I deserve it. I should've used common sense. How do you think did Rose feel when I put her through this pain? I can literally feel and understand how she felt back then and to even think about the fact that she had to endure all of this really breaks my heart and only makes me hate myself even more. The hate she feels towards me is totally justified and I don't even blame her."

"Look, I highly doubt that Rose hates you. She is...different. She's too nice. She may say she hates you, but deep down she doesn't. It's some kind of facade. I bet she doesn't hate you - especially not anymore. I don't know whether it is the right time to say this, but I've seen her a few months ago because I had to see how she was doing in order to move on with my life. Similar situation, huh?" He rubbed his neck, looking at me from the corners of his eyes. "When I visted her we've had some time to talk and guess what she asked me?" A small smile crept over his face. "She asked whether I knew how you were doing. She also asked whether we managed to put our differences aside."

My lips parted as I opened my eyes in shock. "What!?"

"Please just go see her, Miles. I promise you'll feel better once you openly talk to her. I bet she wouldn't want you to feel like this, you know? You need to get help." He was worried about me, I could hear and see it but I didn't want to. I knew meeting and talking to Rose was the only solution for my problems, but I too scared to be confronted with her.

I played with my thumbs, shaking my head. "Did she tell you about her boyfriend?"

He was in deep thought for a second. "Oh, Austin? How do you know about him?"

I scoffed again, "I met him in person."

Andrew leaned forward within an instant while looking at me in utter bewilderment. "What!?"

"He visited me in Pennsylvania. I told my roommate about my past with Rose and he wanted to help me reach out to her, so he basically messaged her boyfriend in my name and...whatever. A couple of days later we met in a small diner and he handed me those unaddressed letters from Rose. I read them - no, I memorized them right here," I said pointing at my head. "She definitely hates me."

"Wait...I'm just trying to deal with the fact that her boyfriend visited you. Don't you think that's weird?" Andrew scratched his neck again as his eyes were roaming around the tiny church. "I mean if I were Austin, why would I visit you? And why would I give you some letters my girlfriend wrote for you? I can't come up with a valid reason."

I shrugged, digging my nails deep into my palm to stop my damn tears from escaping. "I guess he wanted to make me hate myself even more. And that's why I just want to tell her how sorry I am. I just want to look into the mirrow and not hate the person staring back at me. I just want to live my life without all the remorse and all the pain killing me from the inside. I want to get rid of this pain, get rid of all the memories, all the mistakes, just everything. I just want to be happy, Andrew. Truly and genuinely happy."

"Miles..." he put his hand on top of my shoulder to squeeze it. "I see how bad you're doing right now and I can't even imagine how awful you must have been those past three to four years but please stop being so hard on yourself. Accept the past, move on and do better in the future. What keeps you from reaching out for her?"

I hit my fist against a wooden piece in front of me, "I'm too damn scared!"

"Scared? Do you hear yourself talking?" Now he turned his body towards me completely while pushing his eyebrows together in anger.

"You don't get it," I wiped my tears away with the sleeve of my white shirt. "In order to move on, I have to face the past and I'm scared of it. I...I want to feel wanted again, you know? What if my conversation with Rose doesn't go as planned? What if meeting her will ruin me even more?"

"Stop overthinking," he begged. "That's the worst thing to do to your mind."

"If I disappeard right now, how many people would care? One? Maybe two? I want to feel loved again. I want to feel needed again. I want to cross someone's mind again. I want those midnight talks and lazy sundays again. I want to show someone how much I love them but with this state of mind I can't do any of that. I need a hand to pull me out of this."

He jumped up from his previous position and remained silent for a few more seconds until I could see him reach his hand out for mine. "Let me help you out of this. I can't bare to see you ruin your future because of this."

I stared at his pale hand, which was covered with some silver rings and a lion tattoo on his index finger before I shook my head. "You can't help me. I need to pull myself out of this, but I appreciate this gesture."

He laughed, "I know. I said 'let me help you', not 'let me pull you out of this'."

"Can you do me a favor?"

He nodded, "Sure. What is it?"

I opened my jacket to grab something I was hiding in my inner pocket for a couple of weeks now. "Here. This, uhm...is a letter. I want you to give it to Rose."

"Oldschool, huh?" He opened his hand to take it, looking at me with a confused smile. "Why don't you give it to her instead?"

"Because you both live in New York, don't you? And you said you visited her once, so I assume that you know her actual address plus she talks to you." I shrugged, securing my hands behind my back. The letter I had just given to Andrew was the most important piece of paper in my life and I prayed that it would fulfill the deed I wrote it for.

"Okay, how do you know that?" He laughed again, still looking at me confused. "Should I be scared?"

"She once told me that she wanted to live in New York when she's older, so that was a pure assumption," I defended myself.

"And what about me? I never told you about New York."

"Instagram," I shrugged again before we both bursted out in laughter.

It felt really good to laugh again, especially with a person whom I had known my whole life. It felt even better to know that he accepted my apology and gave me another chance to prove that I had changed - which he already pointed out himself. And the best and most rewarding feeling was to know that he didn't judge me because of my past and that gave me some hope for Rose to do the same. Maybe she'd accept my letter and give me another chance to prove that I had in fact become a completely different person.

A tiny piece of hope ignited the small flame in my soul again.

...

author's note:

*I didn't edit/re-read this chapter, so sorry for any typos or sentences that don't make any sense.

Hi peeps, I hope you're all doing great after Christmas! This chapter has been lying in my drafts for a couple of weeks now and I thought I'd release it before 2020, but due to some overthinking, I wanted to edit it and now it's the first update of the new decade, lol. :-)

I actually also have some news for you: I'm thinking about a third book in this 'All Too Well'-series. I'm currently thinking of a short (really, really short) book with only about 6 chapters (including prologue and epilogue). The title will be 'Farewell' (no, this is not a spoiler), but I've had some very cool thoughts about it and now I want to turn my thoughts and aspirations into an actual story. What do you guys think? Would you be down for another book in this series with the same characters? Or would you like to see/read something else?

That's it for now. HAPPY NEW YEAR!!! I hope this year will be a great year filled with happiness, love and positive vibes only. I also hope that this year brings you all the energy and motivation you need to fulfill your dreams.

Thank you for sticking around in 2019, I hope to see you in 2020 as well.

Much love and thank you.

Chapter 23 - Green Day & Reunions...

T ime will tell

"As my memory restsBut never forgets what I lostWake me up when September ends"

- Wake Me Up When September Ends, Green Day

—

"Thank you for not letting me down, I owe you!" I said with happy tears in my eyes as I looked over at Baldwin who was about to fall asleep on the big white sofa in the lobby of our hotel. We had just arrived in New York for the Green Day concert tonight and although Baldwin was feeling awful, he decided to accompany me since the two of us were supposed to attend the concert together before he was forced to cancel due to his ilness.

"I should be the one thanking you," Andrew laughed into the speaker. "Prepare yourself for one hell of a night. Our teenage dream is coming true, baby!"

To attend a Green Day concert has been a dream of mine ever since I've heard them on the radio while driving to a football game with my father when I was about eight. Each time I tried to get a ticket for their concerts, they were sold out already and I truly believed that I'd never see them live. "I'll text you once I'm ready."

"If I have enough time I'll make sure to pick you up - or else we'll just meet at Madison Square Garden, alright?" he asked and I nodded, although he couldn't see me.

"Alright, see you!" I hung up the phone and walked over to where Baldwin was seated to squeeze his shoulder lightly to make sure he was awake.

He sneezed two times in a row before he said, "I am so sorry, Miles. I wish I could come with you, I am seriously not feeling good at all and all these meds give me headaches."

I smiled. "I told you not to worry about it anymore. You should probably just rest."

"Okay," he said hoarsely, cleaning his throat. Once he was ready, I helped him to walk all the way up to our room and made sure to order some camomile tea while he was wrapping himself around his blanket.

"I feel bad for leaving you alone tonight," I admitted. I sat down onto my bed and let out a loud sigh. It was weird to be in New York because I had never thought about coming here at all. I had no idea where exactly Rose was living, but we were practically breathing the same air. I also didn't know how long it had been since we were so close to each other. I walked over to our small balcony and stared out of the window as I drifted into some deep thoughts.

Where are you, Rose?

"I'm okay!" He tried to speak through the blanket, which was now covering his face. "I'll probably sleep for the next 24 hours aynway. Hopefully I'll feel better afterwards."

I didn't really listen to what he was saying because I was already way too focused on my thoughts. I was suddenly wondering whether Andrew already had the chance to see her to give her the letter I had written. Did she read it? What did she think about it? No, she obviously did not read your damn pitiful letter, you ididot! My subconscious shouted at me. She would have messaged or called you if she did. Or perhaps she read it and threw it away because she's over you. Stop thinking about her and move on. Get your life together.

I shook my head. I truly didn't want to believe that she was over me. This small flame of hope inside of me was still burning and I was praying for it to ignite our love as well. She's over you. Move on. I shook my head again, rubbing my temples. She's living her best life without you. She is living her life with a man by her side who makes her feel loved, wanted and appreciated. You only made her feel absolutely awful about herself. You made her feel unloved, unwanted and worthless. She hated herself because of you. Don't you realize it? You were toxic.

I felt the now familiar hot tears in the corners of my eyes. The same tears I was hiding or perhaps holding in for the past three and a half years because I thought crying was for the weak. Cry as much as you want to. It won't change anything. The outcome remains the same. You ruined it - you ruined everything. Now suffer. Be unhappy. Be sad.

"Get rid of those dark thoughts right now," Baldwin shouted just in time as if he was able to read my mind. My head shot sideways immediately and I was grateful that he pulled me out of my thoughts before my mood would drop deep down underground. "Please stop thinking about whatever you were just thinking about. Replace those thoughts with Green Day! Think about how you're going to see Billie Joe Armstrong in less than three hours. Think about how you're going to scream all the songs you've memorized over the last decade at him!"

I couldn't stop myself from smiling widely again. "Thank you, Baldwin."

"Hold on," he said, reaching over to grab his phone. "What was the song called? The one where he sings 'I walk a lonely street...'" he asked, looking at me confused while humming the melody.

I pulled my eyebrows together. "It's actually 'I walk a lonely road'," I corrected, sounding a little offended.

He probably typed in the lyrics because now he was trying to sing, "the only one that I have ever known..."

I just stared at him until he signalized for me to continue. "Don't know where it goes, but it's only me and I walk alone."

"Perfect," he laughed, clapping his hands. "I guess you're ready to go now."

"Thanks, but what would you have done, if you had accompanied me tonight? Do you even know any of their songs?" I scratched my neck. "Boulevard Of Broken Dreams is legendary. I didn't even know that there were people out there who don't know the lyric, let alone the name of the song."

He shrugged, "I guess I would have just pretended to know the lyrics."

A small smile spread across my lips at the thought of the concert. "I can't wait to sing all those songs with the crowd. It's going to be an unforgettable night, I can somehow feel it."

"I'd say record some videos, but I guess you should just enjoy the night and put your phone away until the concert is over." He grabbed a tissue to clean his nose as I nodded in agreement. "I mean one may never know what might happen."

"What do you mean?" I wondered, leaning my back against the wall after securing my hands behind my head.

He put the tissue onto his nightstand before he looked at me again. "Huh?"

"You said 'one may never know what might happen'," I repeated for him. "And I wondered what you meant by that."

Now he was trying his best to just ignore me as he said, "There was no meaning behind it. I can just somehow feel that you'll be quite happy." This time he mocked me and I decided to drop the topic.

...

The word 'excitement' wasn't even close enough to express my feelings in this very moment as I was standing in line at Madison Square Garden. I couldn't even describe this feeling because I never experienced anything as cool as this right here. Green Day was just a couple of minutes away from me and my brain was having a few problems accepting that. I mean once I walked into this huge venue, I would unite with my childhood heroes - the ones whose music had truly saved my life.

I was shaking and my heart was beating so fast and nearly out of my chest that I put my left hand on top of it. I also couldn't really stop myself from smiling like an idiot. For the first time in so long, I felt...happy? This feeling seemed so unfamiliar and new to me that it took me quite a while to get used to it again. Currently Green Day was my only source of happiness. They filled not only my life, but also my empty soul with joy - something I hadn't felt for so long. The fact that I was attending their concert was the only reason that kept me going through life. I counted all those months, weeks and days until today would eventually come.

Although I was aware of the fact that this happiness and joy would only last for as long as this concert, it was still a huge blessing to me. I was happy to put my depressive state of mind and all this anxiety away for a brief moment. I was happy to pretend that everything was going to be okay for a few hours. I was even happy to be me just for this one moment in my life. I closed my eyes and let the happiness soak right into my bones before this sweet feeling would vanish again. I sighed because I wanted to be happy forever. I didn't want to be faced with reality again, didn't want to be sad and hurt again. I simply didn't want to go back living my life in hell once this special trip to heaven was over.

A fist collided with my upper arm and once I opened my eyes, I noticed Andrew with an oversized Green Day hoodie right next to me. "I can practically feel the happiness radiating from you," he joked before we high-fived each other and went in for a hug

"I'm actually quite nervous. We are going to stand right in front of Billie Joe Armstrong. Do you even know what that means? He'll see us. He'll acknowledge us. We're going to be recognized by a legend. Dude, the more I think about it, the more I want to pee in my pants." When Baldwin told me that he managed to get tickets in the 'yellow' circle, which was the area right in front of the stage, I was very close to passing out. He was truly the man and the savior of the day.

"Did you bring a sign that says 'Billie I love you!' or 'Can I get your guitar pick?'" Andrew asked, nudging my ribs with his elbow playfully. "I'm just joking. I know how much they mean to you and I also know that this night is going to be the best one of your life yet. I don't know why, but I have a feeling you'll be a lot happier at the end of the concert than now."

I laughed, shaking my head at his silliness before I had the chance to process the second part of his sentence. "What, why?"

"I don't know, just a guess." I couldn't really figure out what it was, but he was acting suspicious. Andrew loved Green Day, probably not as much as I did, but the reason behind the huge smile on his face was definitely not because of this concert, but because of something else and I was curious to know what it was.

"It's our turn now, come on."

...

Halfway through the show, I had to pull the newly bought grey Green Day hoodie over my head because I was already sweating like crazy. The venue, the people, the atmosphere, the songs and everything about Green Day were absolutely perfect. They were delivering such an epic show that this smile all across my face was breaking records. When was the last time I had felt this happy? Every single soul inside this arena was having the time of their life, including me. Even though I put my phone on flight mode, I decided to record a handful of videos just in case I should ever forget about this feeling of pure happiness spreading through my veins.

My lungs were literally hurting from all the songs I've been shouting at the top of my lungs for the past hours but I truly didn't care. My throat was also running dry and I was slowly losing my voice, but I couldn't stop myself from continuing to sing and scream along with everyone else. Andrew was only singing along every once in a while, but his eyes were sparkling with joy. He spent nearly most of his time with a blonde girl we had just recently met who was about 5'3 tall - or perhaps small. She politely asked us whether she could stand in front of us because of our heights, but her view didn't change at all since the people in front of us were just as tall as us. That's why Andrew offered to put her on his shoulders and she obviously couldn't resist his charm. Now we were singing and screaming alltogether and agreed to eat something once this show was over. She seemed like a nice girl and I had a feeling that Andrew liked her.

When Billie Joe Armstrong grabbed his electric guitar and walked towards the microphone again once he was done, he said, "Turn on the lights, I wanna see you." He paused for a brief moment to look through the crowd and repeated, "Turn on the lights everybody, I wanna see ya. I want to see everybody out there - all the people in the back, come on! This is such a beautiful, beautiful, beautiful night!"

Everyone grabbed their phones and put on their flashlights just as they were told to do. We all clapped our hands, shouted, whistled and just went wild. Due to the guitarist in the back, we could all guess which song was coming next. I was hyped to sing Boulevard Of Broken Dreams at Madison Square Garden with a giant crowd of 20.000 people in New York because this was an experience I'd probably never forget for the rest of my life.

"Shine your light!" He screamed one last time before he finally sang the oh too familiar song. "I walk a lonely road, the only one that I have ever known—" and within a second he turned the microphone towards the crowd and put one hand behind his ear to hear us sing along in unison. I guess this was the last song I could manage to sing at the top of my lungs before my voice would drop, so I put a lot of effort into screaming it out louder than all the songs before.

"Don't know where it goes, but it's only me and I walk alone," everbody shouted, pointing their index finger towards him.

He put the microphone against his lips, "I walk this empty street, now you sing!"

"On the Boulevard Of Broken Dreams!" Andrew and I shouted with a huge smile while looking at each other. The girl on his shoulders was waving her hands from side to side and I was wondering how much stamina he had left in his body to carry her. "Where the city sleeps and I'm the only one and I walk alone!"

The huge smile on Billie Joe Armstrong's face seemed like the reflection of my very own. One could practically feel the adrinaline and happiness racing through his body in a fast pace. What a living legend! This time he placed the microphone stand a few feet away from his body, turned around and waited for us to be completely silent. I was amazed by his ability to control the crowd like this throughout the whole night because within seconds, not a single sound could be heard.

And then he turned towards us and just smirked as he kneeled down to the ground and nodded in satisfaction, while putting his thumb up high like a proud father. Not even a blink later, he jumped back up. "That's how it's done in New York City, baby!" He drove his hand through his messy hair right before the drummer hit the drums and the band began to play the same song again. He sang, "Aha-Aha-Aha-Aha, I'm walking down this line that divides me somewhere in my mind on the border line of the edge and where I walk alone..."

...

"New York!" Armstrong shouted, grinning at us. "You've been amazing! To play at this venue is always a pleasure, but to play in front of a sold out crowd is the greatest feeling in the world. Thank you for deciding to join us tonight. Did you like it?"

Once the crowd roared, whistled and someone a few feet in front of us shouted, "Green Day rules the world!" His lips formed a satisfied smirk and he turned sideways to look at Mike Dirnt. They exchanged a couple of words before he faced the crowd again. "The first time we've played here was in 1994. It's been over twenty years already. Sometimes time flies by pretty fast when you're having the time of your life, am I right?"

"I can't believe it's already over," Andrew said to me with disappointment lacing on his husky voice. "I'll go use the restroom and buy some water. Do you need or want anything?"

I shook my head and didn't even take my eyes off of Billie Joe as I tried to listen to his speech, rather than whatever Andrew had to say.

The lights went off for about thirty seconds, before some blue lights replaced the former white and red ones. I was confused at first, but when I heard the guitar notes, I immediately knew which song they had chosen to close the show with. Wake Me Up When September Ends. A song that had a very special meaning to me now more than ever before. He didn't even sing the first line, but I could already feel a salty tear roll down my right cheek because of all the hurtful memories floading through my mind.

I had to swallow the lump in my throat, as I tugged at my heart again. It hurt to hear him sing those words and it hurt even more because I could feel his pain. I knew that this song was special for him as well. I closed my eyes and just enjoyed this moment right here.

"Summer has come and passed the innocent can never last wake me up when September ends," he sang, sounding quite broken and I whispered along. "Like my fathers come to pass seven years has gone so fast, wake me up when September ends..."

"Here comes the rain again falling from the stars drenched in my pain again becoming who we are." The emotions in this song were so real and touching. One could hear and feel his pain while singing those words out loud. "As my memory rests but never forgets what I lost wake me up when September ends..."

Within mere seconds, my lungs became heavy and I placed my hand around my neck to keep myself from passing out. I suddenly had problems breathing properly and I clenched my chest so tightly.

This could not be real.

This had to be a dream.

This had to be a hallucination.

My breathing became even more rapid and I felt paralyzed.

It all happened too fast.

I blinked once.

I blinked twice.

She was looking over at me - right into my eyes from afar. She was here. There was no single doubt about it. I wasn't dreaming any of this.

Rose was staring directly at me with a surprised facial expression and I had severe problems accepting that. Within seconds I tumbled backwards, trying to regain my balance.

How? What? When? Why?

Do coincidences like this really exist? Does life really have such a funny way of reuniting people in the most unexpected ways? Do things like this actually happen in real life?

My vision went black and I honestly just wanted to get out of here as fast as I possibly could.

—

author's note:

ROSE AND MILES REUNITED AT A GREEN DAY CONCERT! LIFE IS GREAT! (Shoutout to @Trinity018 for guessing this at the beginning of the story. You're the true MVP)

Welp, I didn't plan on writing this chapter so soon because I had a few other things in mind I wanted to write about first before I finally focus on their reunion, but I honestly can't keep up with writing this story anymore. I'm not motivated anymore and I keep running out of good ideas to keep the plot going. That's why I cut about 6 chapters. I guess I have no other choice but to finish this story sooner than I thought.

It's just not fair for you all as well. You keep waiting and asking me for updates, but I always take too long. I'm truly sorry.

I still hope you liked this chapter? If you did, make sure to leave vote and a comment down below.

Thank you from the bottom of my heart.

Chapter 24 - Where Do Broken Hearts Go?

T ime will tell

"Never thought we'd ever have to go withoutTake you over anybody else, hands downWe're the type of melody that don't fade outDon't fade out, can't fade out..."

- Didn't I, Onerepublic

[I highly recommend to listen to the song above after reading the chapter!]

—

I pushed the heavy doors open with my shaking arms and tried to escape from whatever was going on inside this huge arena. Was my mind playing games with me? Was this real? Could it be? How? I honestly felt as if I had just seen a ghost and was in desperate need for answers. This could not be a coincidence. Was this planned all along? Or did my mind mistake another girl for Rose because she looked similar to her? My lungs were running out of oxygen, so I placed my right hand on top of my torso, closed my eyes for a brief moment and inhaled and exhaled slowly.

I shook my head and rubbed my face with both of my hands. Calm down, Miles. I assumed that Wake Me Up When September Ends was the last song of the set because some people were already leaving the venue and I decided to text Andrew that I was waiting outside already. Once I put my phone back inside my pocket, my eyes connected with her again. There was no single doubt about it. This girl was indeed Rose. I felt it once her eyes pierced right through my wounded soul.

I turned around and remained at my spot for a few seconds before my inner-self told me to run away from this. But I couldn't. I felt paralyzed. My legs didn't want to move. It felt as if she had put a spell on me and now I had no other choice than to face her, but I was far from being ready for this. And when my name left her lips, I bit onto my inner cheeks and felt a tear escape from my right eye. "Miles?"

Her voice was so soft and pure, so angelic and calm. There was a small hint of maturity in it, but other than that, she sounded just like her teenage-self. I could recognize her voice anywhere in the world and this was the confirmation I needed to be one-hundred percent sure that it was Rose.

She walked up to me until I could feel her presence right behind me. My lips were trembling because I was trying my best not to cry and I knew that once I looked at her, the tears would be streaming down my face. Neither of us moved. I had no idea what was going through her head, but I knew for sure that this must be just as hard for her as it was for me. She was probably gathering all her strength to make the first move, although I was the one who had to apologize. I was weak. A lot weaker than her. She was strong. A lot stronger than she thought she was.

I exhaled a long breath, wiped my tears away and turned around to finally look at her. My eyes remained closed at first because I was anxious. I was scared to look at the greatest thing that ever happened to me, to look at the greatest thing I had ever known and lost. I blinked my eyes open very slowly and when I finally managed to open them completely, she was looking at me with tears in her eyes as well. I was tongue-tied. I wanted to speak so badly, but I couldn't. My brain was trying to form a coherent sentence, but nothing came out.

I was wondering what was going through her head. I wanted to know what she was thinking about, or how she felt looking directly at me. I wanted her to say something to me. I really wanted to hear her voice again. I wanted to speak with her, wanted to tell her about how bad I was doing without her. I wanted to tell her that Karma was indeed a bitch. I wanted to tell her that I should've cherished her. She was the love of my life and I let her go so easily.

And then the most unexpected thing happened. I opened my arms and pulled her straight to my chest gently with every ounce of courage and strength I managed to gather within the past five minutes. In this very moment I felt more alive than I had ever been. My stomach fluttered at the feeling of her body pressed against mine. She didn't push me away, no, instead she wrapped her arms around me very tightly and let her body sink deeper into me. To have her so close to me again after nearly five years apart vanished all of my worries and I felt safe. Her body felt so familiar to me — the way it fit perfectly to mine, the way it moved, the way she smelled, the sound of her heart beating rapidly...just everything felt right.

When she was in my arms, all of my pain —both mental and physical pain— disappeared. My mind was at peace. It always felt as if the world stopped still on its axis when I was close to her. It felt as if there was not a single soul walking on this earth other than us two. I inwardly thanked God, buried my head in the crock of her warm neck and hugged her very tightly, like a child who didn't want to be separated from his mother. Finally I was back home.

I felt her salty tears soak in my hoodie and her silent sobs fill my ears. My heart couldn't handle this. I stroked her chestnut-colored hair gently as I tried to calm her. "I've missed you so, so much. So unbelievingly much, Rose." My voice cracked and I began to sob as well. This hug was long overdue. Each time a sob left her mouth, she pulled me even closer to her. I could feel my lungs aim for air, but she was all the oxygen in the world I ever needed to survive.

She didn't say anything. Instead she continued to cry and I continued to rub her arms in a soothing way. I had no idea how much longer we would remain like this, but I didn't want this moment to end anytime soon. I didn't want to let go of her. I wanted to remain like this forever because she had the ability to make me feel better about myself. To taste this sweet feeling of happiness again felt so good and I was praying for this to last a little longer.

A small piece of my heart broke when she pulled away slowly to look me deep in the eyes again. She licked her lips and wiped her tears with the back of her small hand as she smiled while shaking her head. She took a small step back and looked away from me. "I really need to talk to you."

I nodded, letting go of her. "I also really need to talk to you."

She grabbed a tissue from her small bag to clean her nose and wipe the remaining tears away from under her beautiful eyes. "I'm sorry you have to see me like this," she apologized. "Let's sit somewhere."

I nodded again, just admiring her beauty. I still couldn't believe that she was actually standing right in front of me. I couldn't believe that we reunited again at a Green Day concert after all these years of being apart.

...

After walking for a couple of minutes, we decided to sit down on a park bench in Central Park. She was walking in front of me and I was basically following her behind in silence. I was still trying to collect my thoughts in order to have an actual conversation with her, but my mind was completely blank. This situation was quite overwhelming and I couldn't seem to relax as my heart was beating like crazy causing my lungs to keep begging for air.

She looked over at me and that's when I once again realized that this right here was indeed happening and not just some random daydream in my head. "Are you not going to speak?"

I turned my head sideways to look at her as well, but whenever my eyes landed on her, I became sad and frustrated because of our past. I opened my mouth to say something, anything, but I still couldn't form a single sentence. I didn't know how I was supposed to apologize correctly if my brain kept acting like this. I would never be able to put my apology into words because it was impossible to make her understand how truly sorry I was from the bottom of my heart. There was so freaking much I had to say, but my tongue was twisted and didn't let me speak.

"I read your letter," she continued. "I probably read it a thousand times. At first, I couldn't believe it was from you...but then I remembered the real you. The real you was not the one you showed to me back then, but the one you decided to hide from me instead. The real you was the hurt and vulnerable Miles. The one who had actual feelings and a heart. The one who was bleeding on the inside because of the knife that was pushed in his innocent heart. I felt your pain so deeply."

So Andrew had the chance to give her the letter I had written a couple of years ago. I was glad that she didn't refuse to take it. I was glad that she decided to keep it and read it over and over again. I was glad that she decided to meet me — even after everything I did to her own innocent heart.

I bit down onto my bottom lip and held back the familiar tears. "You have no idea how many times I wanted to just...disappear once and for all because of all the shit I put you through. My demons still got the upper hand on me. They keep making tempting offers and sometimes I want to take one of those offers, you know? I realized all of my mistakes when it was too late...when you were long gone and not part of my life anymore. Everything I wrote down onto that letter came straight from my heart. I meant every single word I put in it, I want you to know that."

"Miles," she moved closer to me before she continued to talk. "You have no idea how much your letter has meant to me. It helped me to discover who you really are. It helped me to heal. It helped me to forgive."

"You were the best thing that ever happened to me." I shook my head and buried my face behind my hands. "I didn't prove it to you though. I always kept pushing you away from me. I kept hurting you, kept treating you badly. I saw your damn scars and chose to ignore them. I heard your cries for help and I chose to ignore them. I saw you begging on your knees for me and I chose to ignore it. I chose to push you away all the time!" I shouted, "Even when you broke down right in front of me, I closed my eyes and pretended not so see how devastaed you were. I wish I could go back and punsh myself for being such an absolute asshole to you. You honestly have every right in the world to hate me," I said without looking at her anymore. I was angry at my seventeen year old self again. I was by far the most disgusting person on earth. I couldn't believe that I used to be like that.

There was a long silence before she decided to speak up. She was obviously choosing her words wisely because she didn't want to hurt me, but I knew that she didn't feel like this, I mean how could she? "I hated you —or at least I tried my best to do so. But each time I said that I hated you, I hated myself even more for still loving you deep down in my heart. Every sane person would've left, but I couldn't leave you. I knew that you were hurt and in pain and instead of ignoring it, I wantedto help you. Or at least try to. You always had my back and I'm pretty sure that you were aware of that. You took advantage of my good heart."

"And that's why I deserve to die alone," I whispered in front of me as I turned my entire body away from her. I didn't want her to see me like this and most importantly, I didn't want her to lie to my face just to make me feel better about myself. I felt the muscles of my chin tremble like a small child.

She placed her hand on my thigh and tried her best to make me turn towards her again. "Miles, please. That's not what I'm trying to say. You're not that same evil hurt boy anymore. I mean you're obviously still hurt but because of another reason. You've grown so much —both physically and as a person. You've been reflecting all your mistakes for the past what? Three years? Four years? You keep suffering because of what you did to me, but I don't want you to suffer. i did most of this to mysel!" She raised her voice as well. "Your letter was a cry for a help, I could feel it. I could feel your despair, your hopelessness and your pain. I'm here to make you understand that I'm happy again, Miles. I also want to make sure that you're doing good because to suffer alone is the worst feeling in the world. Trust me when I tell you that you don't deserve any of this."

I shook my head, finally letting my tears escape as I said, "It just gets so loud sometimes. The voices in my head get so loud, Rose. I can't bear it anymore." My tired eyes dripped with tears and I felt hollow. My pain was still an open wound that couldn't heal. I broke down entirely and let those hot tears wash away all my defences. I clenched my hands into shaking fists and hoped that there would be some violent solution to my pain...if only I could find it.

This time she grabbed my cold hands in her warm palms and pulled me closer towards her. I finally sobbed into her chest unceasingly, drenching her white shirt with my salty tears. "It will get better, I promise." She rubbed circles on my back with her thumb. "I wish I could've saved you from yourself." Her voice was calm and soothing with a hint of disappointment lacing on it.

I sniffled, "I was looking for an angel who could chase my demons at night and when you were gone, I realized that you were my angel."

"Look at me," she demanded nicely, trying to push me back up.

I ignored her statement and let my eyes stay fixiated on the ground beneath us as my tears dripped down. "I can't. Looking at you hurts too much."

She was stubborn, so she kneeled down right in front of me and this time I had no other choice but to look straight into her beautiful ocean-blue eyes with my swollen and sore ones. They were still as mesmerizing as they used to be. The color that had drained out because of me had returned. They were bright and in living color again. "I left my past right where it belongs. I closed that dark chapter and moved forward with my life. I was stuck in this tiny hole for way too long. I let my life pass right in front of me until someone reached a clean hand out for me to take. Yes, I do have scars on my body. But they keep reminding me of how strong I am. I honestly don't want to be the reason why you're feeling so miserable. It's a never ending circle, Miles. If you stay depressed and won't let people help you, I'll feel sad too. It's selfish of you to do this."

"Rose," I gulped, driving a hand through my already messy hair. "Stop this." My tear-rimmed eyes were burning and my chest felt heavy as if it were filled with lead. My whole face was now washed with a dull red, including the very end of my nose. My throat tightened, so I opened my mouth to let in a small breath.

"Seeing you like this hurts me too, you know? I always wanted nothing but the best for you. Even back when we were sort of dating, I knew that your heart didn't belong to me and probably never would. I knew that your heart only belonged to Josephine. I knew that I could never replace her or be like her... and that's why I prayed for you to either move on and be happy on your own or solve whatever happened between the two of you and be happy with her. That's what hurt the most: to love someone who doesn't love you back." Her voice broke at the end and she inhaled a deep breath in. "Unrequited love is the worst kind of love."

I squeezed her hand lightly. "I'm just so sorry, Rose. I love-"

She cut me off and said, "I'm sorry too...I really need to go, Miles." When she pulled her hand out of my loose grip, I immediately missed the warmth of her hands.

"You deserved better back then, I know. But let me treat you better now, Rose. I'm begging you to hear me out. There is so much I still have to tell you-"

She cut me off again and said, "I really need to go, Miles. I've found my place in this world and I'm sure you will too. You'll find something or perhaps someone who is worth living for. Someone who paints those grey clouds away for you." Were her last words before she turned around to walk away once and for all but she stopped right in her tracks after taking two steps.

"Will I be okay?" I shouted from behind.

When she faced me one last time, her bottom lip quivered and a single pearl-shaped tear rolled down her blushy cheeks. She was trying her best to seem strong in front of me, but I was aware of the fact that neither one of us was prepared for this. Her mind was probably flooded with thousands of hurtful memories from our past each time she looked at me. She was probably thinking about the boy she used to give her all to — the same boy who didn't return her love when she needed him to. I will always remain the dark chapter in her life and sadly, there is nothing I can do about it. "I'll pray for you, so please don't ever lose your faith. I may have lost this battle against your demons, but I don't want you to lose it too. Please don't ever give up."

I felt a stinging in my nose and my throat started to tighten again. I opened my mouth to let in a long breath as tears welled in my eyes. I fought with everything I had to keep them from dripping down. "Rose, please stay," I begged desperately, but when she shook her head and turned away from me I lost it. Peal shaped tears rapidly streamed down my face and I started to whimper like a baby. "Rose please," I begged again. But it was no use.

She walked away and left me standing there, alone. I collapsed to my knees and everything inside me shut down. My eyes stung and my body trembled. "...don't go" I muttered to myself, collapsing completely.

—

author's note:

I hope you enjoyed this chapter!!! I also hope everyone is staying safe AND inside. I'm praying for us all to survive this pandemic. I truly want this to be over...

A vote and a comment are much appreciated.

Much love to every single one of you.

Chapter 25 - If We Had Never Met

Time will tell

"Oh, what I wouldn't give for just a moment to holdBecause I live for this feeling, this everglow."

— Everglow, Coldplay

-

I was still sitting on the cold hard ground with tears streaming down my face over and over again. I hadn't moved a slight bit ever since she left me here on my own because I didn't have any strength left in me anymore. This just hurt way too much. She basically told me to leave her alone in the nicest way possible, but her words still managed to shatter my broken heart into even tinier pieces. I did not deserve her —I never did.

I had no other choice but to surrender. It was over for me here. I had to accept that she chose him and not me. Sadly, there was nothing I could do about it. He made her feel safe, feel loved and cherished. He made her feel all the things I couldn't manage to make her feel when I had the chance to. "I surrender," I mumbled to myself. "Now it's time to move on somehow."

The sorrow drained right through me. I couldn't even find the right words to describe my sadness. It felt like death by a thousand cuts. Every time I remembered what I had lost, another new cut was added to my already wounded and damaged heart. I had a feeling this would never stop. Especially not now or in the near future. I felt hollow. I was a mere shell of what I had once been. It felt as if my inner self was locked in a cage surrounded by my demons and there was no way out. They kept haunting me.

I shook my head, swiping the remaining tears away with both of my hands as I tried to get rid of these dark thoughts and the voices inside my head. My phone was vibrating, but instead of answering, I decided to turn it off. I wanted to be left alone. I wanted to deal with this whole situation on my own. I didn't want people to pity me or tell me to move on because I was already trying my very best to let go of my past. It was just a very hard task and I was aware of the fact that I needed a lot more time than other people probably would.

My mind was trying its best to find a way to live in peace again. But how? I was drained of all hope. The emptiness within me was eating me alive like a hungry rat nibbling at my insides. Rose stole my heart a long time ago and in order for me to move on, she had to return what she had stolen. She already did, idiot. A hundred of times already. Stop looking for reasons to hold on to her with your dear life. She doesn't care about you anymore.

A cold breeze of air hit my face and a shiver ran down my spine immediately. It felt like there was no skin over my pain and the wind just made it bleed. But maybe I was the one who kept poking into my open wounds with a stick to make them bleed again. Why? Because what else was I supposed to do? It felt wrong to be happy, but it sure as hell didn't feel right to drown in my own agony.

You have a lot of invisible scars scratched all across your heart and soul, but you don't give yourself the time to heal. You don't give your body the time to reduce those scars since you keep adding more to your collection. Self-hatred, self-destruction and a low self-esteem. These three ingredients don't let your mind heal and therefore also don't let those scars fade in time someday. If love can fade, then so can all the pain in your heart and mind.

Why did it feel as if my demons didn't want to leave me alone then? Why did it feel like they wanted to bury me alive instead? Because of these thoughts and all the pain I had to endure, I truly never wanted to love anyone ever again. Apparently all you get out of it is loneliness. Love can be the greatest feeling in the world, but it can also damage your soul in the cruelest way. It can break your heart into tiny pieces instead of creating butterflies in your stomach. Unfortunately, this never ending loneliness kept reminding me of Rose and each time she captured my attention, I couldn't stop thinking about her - about her smile, her eyes, her scent, her touches...just everything.

Life became vulnerable as I was enslaved by her thoughts. She was my world and I was the moon revolving around her. She connected with a part of me others couldn't connect with. She saw a light in me no other could see. She saw a part of me and my soul I never wanted anybody to see, a part of me I never wanted to let out of the bag. She saw my dark side and decided to stay right by my side.

"Who would you be if we had never met?" she sobbed to draw breath. When I recognized her beautiful, yet broken voice, I jumped right back up onto my feet within mere seconds. She came back. Although her eyes and the tip of her nose were quite red now and even though her face was covered in tears, she was still trying her best to seem strong. My lungs heaved and I stayed head bowed until I could find the right words to say. I had never thought about this question or perhaps I did, but I never managed to find a pleasant answer. Who would I be?

"If we had never met," I whispered hoarsely, pausing midsentence to think about this question intensely. "I would still be the asshole you met a couple of years ago. If we had never met, I would probably be getting drunk somewhere right now. I would probably be waking up in some strangers bed. I would probably be lost in this world, but most importantly, I would be a completely different person than I am today. I would have separated myself from my family and would be lonely."

My answers didn't satisfy her. They were far from what she wanted to hear, I could see it in her eyes. She licked her dry lips wet right before she tugged her bottom lip between her front teeth and looked up at the sky to make her tears stop somehow. When she turned her head away from me, I tried my very best not to reach out and cup her face in my hands to make her look at me instead.

After a long silence, I decided to speak up and try again. "If we had never met, I would have given up on true love a very long time ago. If we had never met, I would have never known what it feels like to be loved by someone so deeply. I wouldn't have known how sweet love tastes and how good it can make you feel. Rose, if we had never met, I would've forgotten what it means to be happy. You had this certain effect on me no other did. Even during my darkest times, you managed to lift my mood. I know it didn't always work, but—"

She began to shake her head, squeezing her eyes shut. "I'm just so confused. I'm sorry. I shouldn't have returned."

Right when she was about to turn her back on me for the third time today, I grabbed her by her arm gently and rushed in front of her to stop her from walking away from me again. We had to talk. There was way too much I had to say. "Listen to me, please. I'm begging you to hear me out. Please give me a chance to explain myself. I have so much to tell you."

"Miles..." she cried, "don't do this." Suffering, loneliness, longing, desire; her eyes held all those deep seated emotions and many more. She was mortified, scared and anxious, but who was I to judge? I felt the same, but ten time worse.

"I miss you, I miss you so much. You walked out of my life and the gap you left behind just couldn't be filled by anyone else. I miss your body laying next to mine in the morning. I miss your arms wrapped around me so tightly during the night. I miss you stroking my hair while I was falling asleep. I miss your teeth glistening when you smile, or your eyes twinkling with laughter when you hear something funny. I miss everything about you, Rose. Not to see you for four years was tough, but seeing you right now hurts a lot more because it brings back so many memories I am trying to hide deep within me. When you left, this pain sat in my guts like a wildfire burning slow." I grabbed my chest tightly because it ached looking at her tear-streamed face. No one had ever managed to replace her within all these years and no one ever would. "I regret all the bad things I ever said to you, I really do. I wish I could retract all the cruel words I spat at you when I was angry. I gave you only passive aggressive rage, I withdrew to punish you and became self-absorbed."

She was still avoiding to look at me, so I continued.

"You're gone now. You're not mine anymore. You fled to someone else —to someone who gives you all the things I couldn't give to you. You fled to someone who gives you hugs instead of cold stares, listens to your problems instead of ignoring you, shows love and affection instead of condemnation. I'm praying that you can make up for those wasted years we shared. I'm praying that he makes you smile all the time, that he makes you feel happy and cherished every minute of the day. I wish you were still by my side. I- I wish I could make amends. I wish I was still the one you called your lover and that it was still me who you snuggled after dark and in the morning."

Her eyes remained closed, but her tears were still dropping down from her cheeks and I took a small step closer towards her.

"I have grown, Rose. I have grown and learned about what really matters in life, but sadly not soon enough for us."

"You need to move on," she mumbled this time. "This is not fair. Neither one of us deserves this, especially Austin. Let go of me, Miles. Once you erase me out of your mind, you will heal. That's how I moved on."

I scoffed, "Did you really? Then why are you standing here, crying in front of me? Are you sure that you've moved on from me? Damnit Rose, you carved yourself a role right into my DNA and no matter how hard I try to remove it -to remove you- it remains unchanged."

She took a step back from me. "Over time, the memory of your presence has escaped from my mind. You weren't the center of my universe anymore. You gave me millions of reasons to leave you and when I managed to realize what you did to me, I gladly took all of them and left. If we had never met, my life would have been so different. Everything about me would have been different! I'm glad that you finally understand how much pain you put me through, but I don't want you or anybody else to ever feel like that. If we had never met, I wouldn't be walking around with scars all over my soul. You definitely left your mark on me."

I didn't like where this conversation was going. I obviously didn't expect her to break up with Austin and come back running to me, but somehow I was still hoping she would. She didn't give me the signals I wanted to receive and that caused my eyes to burn again. The sobs punched through me, ripping through my muscles, bones, and guts. I was blinking lashes heavy with tears."If getting past the pain means forgetting you, then I choose to suffer my entire life."

"No! You don't have the right to say this. Stop putting me in such a bad position, Miles. You honestly need to see a therapist. I'm begging you to stop torturing yourself with our past. If I could change anything about us, I would erase our past within the blink of an eye. I would erase the moment I fell in love with you. I would erase the moment you got your heart broken. I would erase the moment we met. Don't you get it? I'm happy now. I've never been happier and I've never felt better about myself. As sorry as I am to say this to you, I would never return to you, Miles. I'm way too scared." Each word stabbed me like a sharp knife. Each word felt like a slap in my face. Each word felt like a punch to my guts. I was bleeding. I was hurt.

Brick by brick, my walls came tumbling down. I clasped onto something for support because my entire body was shaking. "I-" She secured her arms around my waist and pulled me in when I was about to collapse for the second time within the past hour. I sobbed into her chest unceasingly as my cries echoed through Central Park. It felt as if my pain was coming in waves: minutes of sobbing broken apart by short pauses for recovering breaths, before I pressed her deeper against me to reduce the pain.

Once she guided us to a bench nearby, I put my head onto her lap and closed my eyes immediately, like a small child who had just woken up from a nightmare and was now guided back to his bed by his mother. "Shhh," she rocked her body back and forth slowly, stroking my hair in a soothing way. "These dark days will pass, Miles. Everything will get better." I felt one of her teardrops rolling dowb my neck slowly.

I was exhausted. I was weakened by my demons. It was hard to keep going because this inner fight with myself had sucked nearly all my strength and power out of me. I hadn't slept peacefully ever since she had left. I didn't even manage to sleep at all. I had to take pills to get at least five hours of sleep a day. My mind was surrounded by too many thoughts and I simply couldn't find a switch to turn them all off. The dark circles under my eyes had gotten worse each day, just like my mental health. Why was everything so heavy?

My eyes were burning from the huge amount of tears I had cried today and I squinted them shut. I didn't want to fall asleep, but my body reacted to her touches in a completely different way. The way she caressed my cheeks lightly and played with my hair put me in another state of mind and I couldn't stop myself from slowly drifting away. I was forcing my mind to stay awake, but it obviously didn't want to listen to me. All the hurt and pain in my eyes stopped or perhaps began to vanish slowly and I felt a sad smile spread on my face.

"Before I met you my heart was wounded, with you it became strong and vibrant, now it is simply broken." Were the last words I mumbled in front of me before I drifted into sleep. This was the first time in nearly four years where I managed to find the damn switch I had been looking for. I turned my thoughts off because in this very moment my mind was at peace.

Sadly, in our sleep we dream of things past, things that will never be again.

-

author's note:

SORRY FOR ANY TYPOS OR SENTENCES THAT DON'T MAKE ANY SENSE.

I've been working on this chapter for a couple of weeks now. I had a completely different chapter in mind, but changed it right before I was done writing it. Sometimes I don't know how I want this story to end, but I'll do what my heart tells me to do.

Is there any certain scene you guys want to see happen? Some of you have a lot of great ideas, so let me know!

If you enjoyed this chapter, please make sure to vote and leave a comment down below.

I love and appreciate you peeps.

<3

Chapter 26 - The Good In Goodbye

T ime will tell

"Gave you so much, but it wasn't enoughBut I'll be alright, it's just a thousand cuts..."

- Death By A Thousand Cuts, Taylor Swift

—

When I was woken up in the morning by a stranger who was strolling through Central Park, I was sad and confused because a certain someone was missing by my side. I remembered falling asleep after resting my head on Rose's lap, but apparently she left once I drifted into sleep. My head was hurting and although she put her small jacket on top of my upper body to prevent me from freezing completely, I felt cold.

I remained at my spot and kept rubbing my eyes while thinking about my previous conversation with her. Why did she come back last night? And why did she leave again this morning? I was hopeful. I really thought that she had changed her mind. I thought that she would give me one last chance to prove that I was indeed the guy she fell in love with a long time ago. I knew that she was scared to trust me again, but this time I wouldn't take her for granted. I would treat her the best way I could.

Maybe you two are just not meant to be, my subconscious reminded. She's happy. Leave her alone and find your own kind of happiness. I was just so confused. What was I supposed to do? Damn, these questions were bothering me ever since I could remember and I was sick of all of this. Sometimes good things have to fall apart, so better things can fall together, I kept telling myself.

I regretted a lot of things in my life. But letting go of Rose was something that I could never forgive myself. Instead of fighting for her or trying to explain myself when her wounds were still fresh and bleeding, I waited for them to heal until I could re-open them and hurt her even more than I probably did back then. What I was doing was unfair. I knew that I didn't have the right to jump back into her life like that, but she was the one who approached me.

She approached you because you reached out to her by writing a letter. She felt bad for you. She pitied you. Even though she's happily in love with someone else, she cares about you so deeply. She always has and she probably always will. That's how she's built. No matter how badly you hurt her, she could never hurt you back, my subconscious remarked again and I sighed. Having conversations with myself was quite exhausting. I kept overthinking everything and that was eating me from the inside.

I grabbed my phone and turned it back on. Once I unlocked it, thousands of notifications about missed phone calls and new messages popped up straight away. There were only two people who would care enough or worry about me to reach out for me, and one of them was someone I had to have a word with. I was aware of the fact that Andrew arranged this meeting with Rose. Coincidences like this don't just happen — especially after a concert — and so I grabbed Rose's black denim jacket and made my way over to Andrew's apartment.

...

Since this was the first time I had come to New York, I had some trouble finding Andrew's apartment directly. I felt like some sort of tourist because I kept asking people about his address and once I managed to find it, I let out a sigh of relief. On my way I also texted Baldwin to come meet me there. I felt remorse for leaving him alone all night, especially because he was sick. Thankfully, he assured that he was feeling a lot better after drinking a thousand cups of tea.

After ringing the doorbell for a few times, Andrew gave me access into the building without asking who I was. The hallway was modest, but elegant and very clean. There were a lot of huge windows surrounding me. The walls were painted beige and had some amazing quotes engraved, which made them look quite nice. This place seemed delightfully luxurious and I truly wondered how Andrew managed to pay the rent since he was still attending University.

The elevator was made of steel and hade a full-length mirror in it. The lighting was intense and when I took a short glimpse at myself, I nearly got a heart attack. My hair was a mess, my eyes were swollen and I had dark circles underlying them. I also smelled — or perhaps stank — like a mixture of sweat and beer because of the Green Day concert and all I wanted to do was to jump into the bathroom and take a warm shower.

I inhaled some air and knocked onto his door with the number 48 engraved on top of it. It didn't take long until Andrew swung the door open with half a smile. He didn't seem surprised since he was probably already expecting me to show up here. "Good morning," he greeted. "Come in."

I didn't hesitate and walked straight inside. He motioned for me to walk forward, but I still decided to follow behind as he entered the living room area. I took a small glance around the highly decorated room and enjoyed the atmosphere it provided. Everything seemed expensive and vintage, yet again making me wonder how he could afford these. The room was full of art and some beautiful white flowers. There even hung some polaroids above the fireplace and I had to admit that this place felt like home.

When I was done observing this room, I turned around to face him. "Is there anything you'd like to tell me?" I wasn't angry or mad at him. I was just sort of disappointed and hurt because he could've told me. I was literally caught off-guard and was not even prepared for Rose and I to meet again under these circumstances. "I mean if you would've told me that she wanted to meet me, I would have still said yes. The only difference is that I would have been informed."

He pushed his eyebrows together and turned his lips upside down. "I apologize. You're absolutely right. I should've told you but in that moment I... I promised her not to tell you because she wasn't a hundred percent sure about it."

I shook my head, rubbing my temples. "I'm so mad at myself. There was so much I had to tell her, but I couldn't find the right words to express myself and my feelings. My brain stopped working properly when I saw her. I felt paralyzed. It all happened so fast. One second she was there and the next she was gone. We had some time to talk, yet I still feel like we didn't exchange any words at all."

He nodded understandingly, squeezing my shoulder tightly. "As long as she accepted your apology, there is nothing holding you back from moving on. The sun should be able to shine right through those gray clouds from now on."

"I guess—" I was cut off by the doorbell before I even had the chance to speak.

Andrew was leaning against the doorframe and looked confused. "I wasn't expecting anyone."

"That should be Baldwin. I told him to come meet me over at your place. I thought we could have breakfast together and go stroll through New York before we leave tomorrow," I informed.

"Great idea," Andrew said, walking over to open the door. "I wish you would've stayed longer.

"Don't worry, we'll come visit you again soon! Pennsylvania is not too far from New York, we'll work something out. I've definitely missed hanging out with you," I admitted truthfully.

"So did I. The next time we see each other, I'll introduce you to my peeps. I bet you'll love them and maybe—"

This time Andrew was interrupted by a loud voice. "Andrew!" I heard someone shout from the hallway and within seconds, I recognized who this voice belonged to. Andrew and I looked at each other in shock and awe because he was the last person either of us had expected to show up here. "Where is Miles?"

My muscles tensed and I balled my hands into fists in order to stay calm. "Right here."

Andrew was trying his best to block his view, but he pushed him aside and rushed over to where I was standing. Our last encounter didn't go well. He despises you, Miles. You're trying to steal his girlfriend. You're trying to ignite a fire that has burnt out already. He's aware of it. Maybe you should leave. I won't leave, I replied to my subconscious. I was already preparing myself for a verbal fight, because I didn't want to get into a physical one - especially with him.

"Who do you even think you are?" His face was so close to mine that I could practically feel his breath on my face. "Why did you come to New York? Do you really think I'm that stupid?"

I took a step back to create a widee gap between us and drove a hand through my messy hair. "What's your problem this time?"

He scoffed, tugging at his blonde hair. "What my problem is? You have the audacity to ask what my problem is?" He emphasized out loud. "You! It's obviously you! What was that stupid letter about? Are you seriously trying to lure my girlfriend around your finger again? Does she still look like the weak girl you ruined? Does she? Because I can assure you that she's gotten so much stronger. Get that into your head already."

I shook my head, letting out an exasperated sigh. "I had to talk to her, okay?"

"You destroyed her," he shouted before he covered his face with both of his hands while pretending to be outraged.

I nodded slowly as I closed my eyes for a brief moment to collect my thoughts and to stay calm. "That's right. I did. I destroyed her and guess what? That destroyed me even more."

"You broke a perfectly good heart," he stated the obvious again.

"And that broke me completely," I mumbled hoarsely. He was making me angrier each passing second he opened his mouth and I was getting sick by just staring at him and listening to him talk about what Rose and I had although he didn't even have a clue about us.

"Are you serious? No, you can't be. You didn't even love her, let alone care about her a slight bit. She suffered so much because of all the things you put her through and—"

"Arg, shut up!" I screamed this time because I couldn't listen to his words any longer. "I know that I put her through hell, I know that I hurt her, I know that I made her feel so much pain. I am aware of that, but don't you dare tell me that I didn't love her! You don't know about us, you don't know anything about—"

"I don't want to! I know everything I need to know about you and that's enough. You are pathetic and I am honestly just disgusted by you." It was his turn to cut me off now and once he finished his sentence, I balled my hands into two fists because my anger was boiling inside of my body. I would feel a lot better if I punshed him and broke his nose or knocked him out while doing so, but I couldn't do this for the sake of Rose.

I exhaled out loud, rubbing my eyes before I lowered my gaze on him. "Time will tell."

"What do you mean?"

"Time solves most things. Time heals nearly all of our wounds. Time makes us understand what's important in life, it has a beautiful way of showing us what truly matters," I muttered loud enough for him to hear. "Only time will tell."

"You should leave," Andrew chimed in from behind. "You've said enough."

Austin turned around but stopped right in his tracks. Once he sorted his mind, he faced me one last time. "If you love Rose, then you should let her go," he said with a calm voice this time. "It was a hard task to teach her to love herself again. It was a very hard task to make her understand that she is important and that her life matters. She hit rock bottom when I met her. She was a dead soul walking around. Her eyes were drained of color, they seemed so lifeless. I offered my hand and she didn't turn it down. I love Rose with everything I am and I know that she's happy with me. I'm concerned and I'm freaking scared to lose her, so I'm begging you to stop reaching out for her, Miles."

His words had a certain effect on me. Suddenly, I felt extremely bad and so much remorse. In order for me to understand where he was coming from, I had to put myself into his shoes and once I did, I could not be mad at him anymore. He was acting the same way I would probably act if I were him. He was protective and scared. He loved her so much that he didn't give up on her during her darkest times. He was right by her side throughout her healing process and that's why they shared such a special bond.

As poetic as it may sound, he saved her. He glued the broken pieces back together and made her realize how much she is actually worth. He was her savior, her knight in shining amor - her anchor in life. No matter how hard I'd try to, I could never break their bond, simply because it was too strong to be broken by me. They loved each other and I had no other choice but to respect that.

As long as she is happy, I'm happy.

I didn't have a right to manipulate their relationship. "I'm...I'm sorry, Austin. You are absolutely right. I've had the chance to talk to her and trust me when I tell you that she feels the same way about you. She loves you a lot more than you think. You two are meant to be. I appreciate all your effort in helping her conquer all the messed up things I put her through. Thank you." I surrendered.

Maybe this was the only right decision in my life for the past years. It hurt, but I knew that what I was doing was the right thing to do. Rose was in love with him and vise versa. She found the perfect guy who could give her everything I couldn't give to her. There is no place for me in her tiny world. I simply didn't belong into her life anymore.

I had no idea how our conversation turned from screaming, hatred and jealousy into this within minutes, but I was relieved about it. As much as I tried to deny it, Austin was a good guy. Rose was definitely in safe hands.

He patted my shoulder and shot a smile my way, mouthing a thank you before he finally left. My heart was still aching, longing to fly again. My heart wanted to stretch its wings and soar, and see the vast possibilities of life laid out before her. My heart wanted to beat double time out of love and pure joy. But sadly, it stayed locked up in it's frozen prison, too afraid to pick the lock or try to break the bars instead.

"Are you alright?" Andrew asked after a few minutes of complete silence. "I don't know whether you want to hear this, but I think you did what's best for all of you. I'm proud of you, Miles."

I blinked my tears away, staring at the rose tattoo on my wrist. "I know," I whispered, stroking the spot I fixiated my gaze on. "It's time to let go."

Andrew pulled me in for a hug. "There is a good in goodbye for a reason, my friend. And I'm pretty sure that you'll realize it sooner than you think."

Only time will tell, I reminded myself.

—author's note:

THE NEXT CHAPTER IS GOING TO BE THE EPILOGUE!!!! I'm gonna go cry :-(

I AM SORRY FOR ANY TYPOS OR SENTENCES THAT DON'T MAKE ANY SENSE. I DID NOT REREAD BEFORE PUBLISHING.

How do you like this ending for Miles?

I know that some (or most) of you wanted Rose and Miles to get back together, but I honestly think that wouldn't have worked out. They have such a dark past and... I don't know. I'm sorry for everyone who expected another ending, yet I still hope you enjoyed this one too.

Good news: I might write an alternative ending someday in the future if you guys would like me to. :-)

A vote and a comment are much appreciated.

I'm sending much love to every single one of you.

Chapter 27 - Rose's POV: What's Past Is Past

T ime will tell

I unlocked the door to my apartment with shaking hands and prepared myself for the worst, but once inside, I couldn't notice Austin anywhere. His keys were missing and the bed was untouched. Did he not sleep last night? I had turned my phone off during the concert and didn't think about turning it back on when it was over. Other than attending the concert, my main purpose was to see Miles. I just had to see him, had to talk to him.

I walked to my wardrobe and grabbed some shorts and one of Austin's many shirts before I rushed over to the bathroom and took a warm shower. I had some time to think about last night and couldn't seem to get this vulnerable image of Miles out of my head. I had never seen him like that. He showed remorse and I could practically tell that he had changed quite a lot. He was definitely not the same ruthless boy anymore. And I was very happy about it - I was happy for him.

I was glad that he managed to understand the damage he had caused by his stupid actions. But that didn't mean that he deserved to suffer like he did, especially for so long. I didn't want him to be sad or in so much pain because of what he did to me. I did most of it to myself anyway. If I had the chance to turn back time, I would have probably not even fallen in love with him in the first place. I should've known my worth before I agreed to be his rebound. The more I thought about it, the more I realized that I was the one to blame. What he did was still beyond messed up though.

Yet I learned to move on and was praying for him to do the same. I was living a completely different life today and didn't have any room left for him anymore. Sadly, he'll always have a place in my heart since his name was engraved deep into my soul. I could never forget the pain he caused my innocent heart to endure when I was so young and naive. Nevertheless I have accepted his apology and that really managed to soothe the pain in my chest. I knew that this would be the only right decision to do.

Andrew told me about Miles' current condition and as much as I tried not to show it, I felt bad about it. And when he came up with this Green Day concert idea, I couldn't say no. I knew that I was the only one who could save him from himself. I needed to help him. I needed him to move on and let go of our past. There was nothing he could do to change the outcome of the mess he had created. We had to accept the past and keep moving on.

Once I got out of the quick shower, a shiver ran down my spine. I grabbed my brush and combed my wet hair before I walked back into the bedroom and jumped straight into our bed. I was very tired, both mentally and physically since I couldn't sleep throughout the whole night. I was wondering what Miles would do once he woke up and realized I was gone. I was just hoping that he'd understand the message and stop reaching out for me from now on - I didn't mean it in a harsh way, but I was still hoping that he would understand that there was no future for us anymore.

I closed my eyes and drifted into sleep right away.

...

I was woken up by a hand stroking my semi-wet hair and placing a kiss on top of my head. I blinked my sleepy eyes open and recognized Austin, who was about to leave again but I grabbed his hand and pulled him back down to his previous position. "Hey," I said hoarsely as I adjusted myself. "Where have you been?"

He avoided to look at me as he said, "Where have you been, Rose? I was so worried about you. You could've texted me." He wasn't angry, but rather disappointed and I couldn't blame him because if I were him, I'd probably feel the same way.

"I'm sorry. It's just...there was something I needed to do for myself and a friend. I hope you understand." I leaned back against the headrest and exhaled out loud as I also avoided to look at him this time. I was debating whether I should tell him about Miles or not and although I didn't want us to argue, I knew that I had to tell him.

"It includes Miles, doesn't it?" he asked and my head shot up straight away.

"How-" I cut myself off just staring at him confused. How did he know?

"Honestly? Pure speculation. You told me about his obsession with Green Day and when you were missing the whole night, I thought that he was there as well. Then I stumbled upon his letter and read about his desire to see you again. I called Andrew and he told me that you were fine, so I visited him an hour ago and guess who I saw?" From the sound of it I could tell that he was very disappointed. I should've just been honest to him. I knew that he would've been strictly against it, but at least he would've heard it from me first.

I played with my thumbs because I felt quite guilty. "I'm so sorry, Austin but we really just talked, I swear. I had to see him in order to close that chapter once and for all. He begged for forgivness and I couldn't say no. He was going through a lot and needed my hand to pull him out of that mess. He showed remorse and told me about how much he suffered for the past three years and-"

He pulled me into his chest. "It's okay. I've had the chance to talk to him as well. He seems like a good guy now. I couldn't even spot an ounce of the devil in him. He basically surrendered and now I'm sure that he'll learn to move on from his past. But there's one more thing I need to confess to you."

I pulled my eyebrows together in confusion. "What do you mean?"

He scratched his neck. "I visited Miles a couple of months ago."

"You did what!?" I nearly shouted.

"He messaged me." He said, grabbing his phone out of his pocket and searching for whatever he was looking for. "Here." He turned his phone towards my direction and handed me the device in his hands.

I took it and read the message out loud. "Hey, Miles here. I'm not sure whether Rose has told you about me, but I would like to meet you if that's okay. Message me and we can arrange a meeting."

"Since I knew who he was, I was kind of caugh off-guard. I kept wondering why he wanted to meet me. I mean how did he even know about me? He must've been stalking you on social media and that's when my jealousy hit. I was scared of losing you. I was scared that he might manage to take you away from me. So I did what I thought was the only way to keep him away from you: I grabbed a few of your unaddressed letters and visited him in Pennsylvania. We didn't talk much. I handed him the letters and left straight away." He tried to explain himself and although I should be mad at him for keeping this from me, I couldn't be.

"I think we're even now." I smiled. "I understand why you acted that way, but you should've known that nobody has the strength to pull me away from you."

"I know, I know. It's just...you were acting strange ever since you stumbled upon that box in the attic and I got anxious. I wanted to protect our relationship, but I'm still sorry for keeping this from you." He secured his hands around my waist and pulled me in for another hug.

I closed my eyes and blinked the tears away as I pressed him even deeper into me. "I love you, Austin. I always have and I always will."

He placed another kiss onto my forehead an smiled while securing my messy hair behind my ears. "I've never doubted that. I'm glad that you managed to make peace with your past, that's a very important step in order to let go of it completely. I knew that this uncertainty was eating you alive, but now we can fully focus on our future and all the great things ahead of us. You are the girl of my dreams and I'm head over heels in love with you."

I smiled whole-heartedly as I nodded. "Thank you for being so understanding. That's the reason I fell in love with you in the first place. You always listened to me without judging any of my actions. Now my head is empty and I can sleep peacefully at night."

He leaned in for a passionate kiss and I pressed my lips against his eagerly. For the millionth time since we have been dating, I could feel butterflies errupt from the pit of my stomach and my heart beat twice as fast as it usually did. Like he said before, to me, Austin was also the man of my dreams. I couldn't imagine a life without him anymore. He was too precious and I'd never let him go.

And to you Miles, I wish you nothing but the best on your way to recovery.

Epilogue

8 months later...

Sometimes people are not meant to be. I've experienced this two times already. Sometimes you love someone with your whole heart, but you realize it way too late and then there's no time for you to fix things anymore. I've experienced this once. And sometimes, people fall out of love with you and fall in love with someone else instead. Sadly, I've experienced this twice as well. It hurts a lot because you keep wondering: why ?

I've had a lot of time to think about my past. I've had a lot of time to stop and rewind all the wrong I've done. I've had plenty of time to wonder about the 'what if's'. I've spent a lot of time just praying for this torture to be over, praying for better days to come, praying for the sun to shine on me again. I was convinced that God didn't want me to be happy ever again because of what I did to Rose Johnson. She didn't deserve any of the cruel things I did to her. She didn't deserve to feel unworthy. She simply didn't deserve to feel as if she was not enough because she was more than that. I hurt somebody who loved me despite my many, seemingly unforgivable faults and that messed with my head.

I was blinded by revenge and once I could see clearly again, I realized the aftermath of what I did. I ruined her life, her senior year, even her future. When I left for college, all I could think about was her current condition. I kept wondering whether she managed to move on from me, whether she managed to heal or whether she was still on the verge of giving up. She kept haunting me - even in my sleep. My brain was locked in a cage surrounded by painful memories torturing me all day and all night. Rose Johnson was the one holding the keys to free my mind but she left me locked up in that small cage instead of rescuing me from my demons.

I've learned, I've grown and I've eventually managed to move on with my life. I kept chasing a girl who was happy now. I kept chasing a girl who didn't need me by her side anymore. I kept chasing a girl who was deeply in love with someone else. I had no other choice but to let go. I also learned to accept the fact that I would forever remain the dark chapter from her past and there was nothing I could do about it. Before she took her belongings and left my heart once and for all, she finally unlocked the dark cage I was stuck in for so long and my brain was reunited with freedom again.

When I managed to let go of my past, I felt clean again. I rediscovered who I was. I rediscovered the me that was purely myself. I felt like my fifteen year old self, who had a lot of love to give. I learned to be happy about the small things in life, learned to smile a lot more and eventually learned to enjoy life again. I also remembered that solitude is a form of personal peace and that helped me a lot.

"You look good." Baldwin commented as he leaned against the doorframe. "That shirt was made for you."

I turned around within an instant and smiled. "Thank you. Which one of these shoes should I wear?" I asked, pointed towards my many shoes spread all across the floor. "And which one of these should I apply?" I asked again, pointing towards my newly brought fragrances. I was very nervous and quite excited for today because I had a date. This was my first date in almost five and a half years and that's why I wanted it to be perfect.

"You should go with the ones you're currently wearing. Oh and apply either one of these two." He grabbed both the Armani and the Dior bottle and brought them to his nose to inhale both scents. "Definitely this one."

I nodded, rushing over to grab the Dior bottle out of his hand and threw it onto my bed before I rushed back inside the bathroom to shave my face and take a quick shower. I was scared to be late, but I still had plenty of time left before I'd have to go pick her up. Stay calm Miles, I kept reminding myself.

...

I inhaled a sharp breath in, adjusted my shirt and cleared my throat before I knocked onto the door that lead to her dorm. My palms were sweaty from holding onto the bouquet of flowers so tightly and I was just praying not to start sweating since I was wearing a white shirt. I took a step back when Ally swung the wooden door open and was left speechless.

I gasped, pushing my eyebrows up in amazement. "Wow. You look absolutely stunning."

She licked her nude lips and tried to hide her face behind her small hand. "Thank you, Miles. You're looking quite handsome yourself."

I smiled, shaking my head in embarrassment. "I bought these for you." She grabbed the bouquet of flowers from my hands carefully and brought them to her nose. She closed her eyes and inhaled the smell of the pink roses. "I hope you like them."

"This is such a cute gesture, I appreciate it." She seemed happy and that caused me to let out a sigh of relief. "How did you know that pink roses were my favorite?"

I looked past her and saw her roommate Olivia shooting a huge smile my way, so I returned a smile as well. "Let's just say I'm very good at guessing." Olivia has become a good friend of mine over the course of the past months. She introduced me to Allison in the first place because she thought we were quite similar. And when we all hung out once, I felt a fire ignite in my heart straight away. "Shall we?" I asked, holding my hand out for her to take.

She nodded, bringing the flowers to her chest. "Bye Olivia!" When she closed the door and turned around to face me again, her gaze landed on my bare hand and a huge smile spread acorss her face before she intertwined her small hand with mine. Each touch made me fall for her a little harder and my heart beat a little faster.

"Are you hungry?" I asked, jumping into the car after making sure that she entered the vehicle safely. "I haven't eaten anything the whole day, so I could definitely use some meat right now."

She laughed, staring at me from the passenger seat. "I usually eat a lot during the day, but I also haven't eaten much today. I was way too excited and spent the whole day getting ready for our date." I met Ally a little less than five months ago when I was studying for my exams with Olivia. When she joined us, I couldn't really focus on anything else but her presence. She knocked me off my feet the minute she decided to enter my life and ever since then, I felt more alive than ever.

"I'm sure that you'll love the place I'm taking you to. I've been there a lot lately and trust me when I tell you that they have the best food this city has to offer." I focused on the road ahead but made sure to turn sideways to look at her every once in a while. She looked absolutely breath-taking and I felt very lucky to have the chance to get to know her.

"At this point, I'd probably eat anything so it's totally fine." She joked, pushing my shoulder lightly. "You smell so good," she complimented out of the blue.

I laughed, "Thank you."

"Can we listen to some music?" she asked, grabbing the aux cord. "If you have any oldschool CD's we can listen to them as well." Her question took me back to the day I decided to take Rose to the beach. I remembered how she stumbled upon my blink-182 CD and how we spent the remaining car ride singing All The Small Things from the bottom of our lungs.

The memory of that day made me quite happy and caused me to smile to myself before I shook my head. "I don't have any CD's in my car anymore. Feel free to choose a song you'd like to listen to."

...

"I've had such a fun night." She admitted once we came to a halt in front of her dormroom. "Thank you very much."

I was still very nervous and scared that I might've done something wrong or that she might not have enjoyed the date as much as I did. "Did you really?" I wondered.

She nodded, taking a step towards me to close the gap between us. "I haven't had this much fun in a while. I'd definitely love to do this again. Maybe we could go to the Pier next time and eat some cotton candy."

Her words just made me smile all over again. "I'm down for that."

I could feel my heart beating in my chest as we both remained silent and just stared deep into each others eyes. Her face was only a few inches away from mine and I felt hopeless. I didn't know what to do. Should I listen to my heart and place my lips on top of hers? Or should I listen to my brain and wait until we move further in this friendship? I was convinced that she could hear my heartbeat because she placed her palm on top of my chest and smiled up at me before she grabbed my sweaty hand and put it on top of her own chest as well.

I was surprised when I felt her rapid heartbeat against my palms. "Who's heart is beating faster?" I whispered, leaning in this time.

She chuckled, "I think we'll find out soon."

She leaned in as well, so that her forehead rested against mine. We both closed our eyes and felt our breaths shaking. Her big lips gently brushed against mine - not innocently, like a tease but hot, fiery, passionate and demanding. Even her smell flooded my senses now and I could feel my face flush warm and the hairs on my neck stand. For the first time in forever my mind was locked into the present — this was a very good sign.

Finally my lips touched her plump ones. Sparks flew in every direction, and the world was slowly disappearing around us, along with all of our worries, our troubles and our problems. She made me feel like none of that mattered. We kissed tentatively, passionately and then, tenderly. I honestly never knew a kiss so innocent could be so intimate and electrifying. Her lips were moving in perfect sync, my hands feeling her waist; I pulled her closer to deepen the kiss and make it more passionate.

My hand rested below her ear, my thumb caressing her cheek as our breaths mingled. She ran her fingers down my spine, coaxing shivers out of me and I tried my very best not to let out a moan since we were still standing outside her dorm. I exhaled through my nose, not wanting to let go. She pulled me even closer until there was no space left between us anymore and she could feel the beating of my heart against her very own chest.

I pulled away slowly to catch my breath and to stare deep into her enchanting eyes. "Ally?" When she looked at me it was as if every ounce of breath was taken from my lungs. There was something in those olive green eyes that was so beautiful, so safe and warm. In just one look I was "home." I recalled the day our bond was forged. It was like being let into the warmth after a lifetime of winter.

"Mhmm?" She hummed as she waited for me to continue but I was still busy searching for the right words to say. I had no idea how I should tell her that I was head over heels in love with her. Her chest was rising and falling in such a fast pace that I was scared she might pass out.

I placed my hand on her waist and drew her closer to get rid of the gap between us. I saw her eyes sparkle and her lips curved up into a smile and I couldn't help but smile back. For so long I had longed for this, and now I couldn't bare to lose it - lose this thing that made me feel so complete again. "Falling in love with you feels like entering a house and finally realizing I'm home, Allison."

I feel blessed for the time we had, for the love we shared, and trust me when I tell you that the best of you will always remain in my heart, Rose Johnson. Even though I travel onward with another, I loved you very much.

THE END.

—